# A Lighthouse Christmas

## A CHRISTMAS NOVELLA

### GULF COAST GETAWAY BOOK 3

### BEBE REED

LADYBUGBOOKS, LLC.

# Chapter One

The lights twinkled atop the small wooden structures that had been erected in the only park that Sugar Cove had. Inside the structures, craftspeople displayed their wares—from Christmas-themed sweatshirts to hand-carved manger scenes with each character painstakingly whittled from wood.

Ginny ran her fingers over a particularly beautiful Mary gazing down at the baby Jesus as a voice caught her attention.

"Your hot chocolate, madam."

She glanced up and grinned into Aiden's smiling face. His eyes crinkled in the corners when he smiled at her, and she greedily took the steaming cup of cocoa and sipped it.

Thick, rich chocolate slid down her throat. "Mm. That's delicious. Thank you. What's your secret?"

He thumbed behind him. "My secret is that guy back there."

Ginny glanced around him and spotted a small hot chocolate stand, where a tall man was dipping a ladle into a Crock-Pot and filling Styrofoam cups before passing them out to shoppers.

"Well, that guy is serving up a mean cup of chocolate."

Aiden slid his hands into his pockets. "I like to think I had something to do with it."

"Oh yeah?" she teased. "You mean besides handing the cup to me?"

"It's hard work walking over here while holding the cup. It got heavy," he joked.

She chuckled. "I'm sure it did."

Aiden exhaled and surveyed the many shops. "So, where would you like to start first? Who's on your list?"

He glanced down, trying to sneak a peek at the small notebook-sized slip of paper in her hand. "Oh no you don't. You don't get to look and see if you're on here."

"I don't? Why do you have to take all the fun out of shopping?"

"Because then it wouldn't be a surprise."

He slung an arm over her shoulder. "Okay, then. We'll shop for your daughters, and I'll carry all the bags."

The closeness made his leathery scent trickle up her nose. It was warm, familiar, comforting. "Great, because I'm going to need all the help I can get carrying gifts."

"That's what I'm here for," he joked.

She was about to reply when a new voice caught her attention. "Ginny, have you been here long?"

She glanced over to see her best friend, Farrah, crossing to her. Farrah had blonde hair that hung in big barrel curls over her shoulders. She wore a deep red sweater and slimming jeans. Beside her was Reece, Ginny's youngest daughter. Reece had a scarf wrapped around her neck, and she smiled when she spotted her mother.

"Aiden and I just arrived," Ginny replied to Farrah. "Thought we'd get some Christmas shopping done."

"Correction," Aiden said, "I'm not doing any shopping. I'm only here to carry bags."

Ginny nudged him playfully with her elbow. "That's a very important job, too."

"Oh, it is," Farrah agreed. "When I Christmas shop, there are always tons of bags. Of course, there may not be as many this year since I'm on my own."

Farrah's face fell and Ginny rubbed her shoulder. "Come on, now. Things'll work out."

Aiden squeezed Ginny's arm. "I'll be right back. There's someone I need to talk to."

Ginny suspected that there wasn't anyone he needed to see, he simply wanted to give her and Farrah some room to speak. "Have you talked to Brad lately?"

Farrah sighed. "What's there to say?"

Farrah had appeared on Ginny's doorstep Thanksgiving Day, declaring that her husband was cheating. Ever since then she'd been staying at the lighthouse, where Ginny lived.

"It's Christmastime," she told her friend. "You should talk to him."

"Yeah, Aunt Farrah," Reece added. "Maybe this is all a big misunderstanding."

Farrah's eyes narrowed. "It's not a misunderstanding. He's cheating. I know that for a fact."

"But you didn't catch him in the act," she reminded her friend.

"Well no, but I know that he is." Farrah rolled her eyes. "I've been married to that man for over twenty years. Something was off. He didn't deny that when I confronted him."

Ginny pointed toward one of the booths. "Let's shop while we talk."

Farrah and Reece followed, but Farrah's face was pinched, her lips turned down in a sulky pout. Ever since Farrah had arrived, she'd insisted that Brad had been cheating, but as far as Ginny knew, there hadn't been any concrete evidence of that, and Farrah wouldn't talk to Brad to work things out.

"I'm saying this for your own good," Ginny said as she rubbed a soft sweatshirt between her thumb and forefinger, "you need to talk to your husband. It's Christmas. You can't ignore the man."

"I'm not ignoring him."

"Aren't you?"

Farrah scoffed. "Yes, he's called."

"Have you said more than one word to him?"

"Why should I?"

Ginny dropped her hand from the sweatshirt and studied her friend. Farrah picked up a hanger with a dark silver blouse on it and pressed it to her torso. "How do you think I'd look in this?"

"Fabulous, of course," Reece said.

"Maybe I should wear it to our divorce meeting."

Ginny's mouth dropped. "Have you filed for divorce?"

"No. I haven't filed for anything. Neither has he. I don't understand

3

what he's waiting for. I've made it perfectly clear that I'm not going back to him."

"Maybe he hasn't filed because he didn't *do* anything," Reece murmured.

Farrah's jaw fell. "Of course he did something. That man was cheating, and that's all there is to it."

Ginny shot Reece a look. She wasn't sure if she believed that Brad had cheated on Farrah. He'd denied the allegations, as most men would. But she'd known him for over twenty years. He was a good father, a good husband.

"All I know is that I'm not going back to him."

"Back to who?"

A tingle ran down the back of Ginny's neck as she glanced over the rack of clothes she was shopping. Standing on the other side, staring down at Farrah, stood Brad—her husband.

He was tall. He'd been a basketball player in high school, so he was *that* sort of tall. He wore a light wool coat that was buttoned to his chin. His short gray hair was brushed to one side, and his brown eyes were fixed with intensity on his wife.

Farrah dropped the blouse she held. Brad slowly bent down and picked it up, hanging it back on the rack.

"Brad," Farrah gaped. "What are you doing here?"

"Well, when you wouldn't return my calls, there was no other choice except to track you down."

Farrah's head whipped toward Ginny. "Did you know about this?"

"No. Of course not."

"There's only one Sugar Cove," Brad told her. "It wasn't hard to find."

Farrah watched him closely for a moment before she lifted her nose. "Well, you've made the trip for no reason because I'm not coming back. Not after what you did."

People turned to look in their direction. Ginny cleared her throat lightly. "Perhaps y'all should take this conversation someplace more private. That is, if you don't want all of town to know your business."

"That's a great idea," Brad said. "Farrah, can we talk?"

The earnestness in his voice made Ginny's heart crack in two. "He's come all this way," she coaxed.

Fire lit in her friend's eyes. "Whose side are you on?"

"I'm on the side of truth," she told her.

"So am I." Farrah shook her head and closed her eyes. "I appreciate you coming all this way, but you shouldn't have. This doesn't change anything. I know what I saw. I know what you did. You can't lie to me."

"Farrah, please," he started.

"No."

Brad's face fell, and Ginny shook her head, not believing that her best friend could be so selfish. Well, if Farrah wasn't going to talk to him, then at least Ginny would.

"Come on," she said, pulling him away from the clothes and stepping out into the Christmas market with him. When they were out of earshot, she said, "I'm sorry you came all this way to see her and she won't talk to you."

Pain laced his voice. "This isn't like her not to talk to me. What'd she say happened?"

Ginny turned back to look at her friend, but Farrah wasn't watching them. She'd tugged Reece into another shopping stall. "She was very vague."

Brad shook his head. "I can't understand why. You're her best friend, Ginny, and I'm not going back until she comes with me. This is all a big misunderstanding, and I'm going to convince her of it."

She patted his arm. "I'll try to talk to her, but honestly"—she sighed heavily—"Farrah hasn't talked much. She mostly just works and keeps herself busy."

He rubbed the back of his neck. "Well like I said, I'm not going anywhere. I've taken time off from my job, and come hell or high water, Farrah's going to talk to me."

She smiled encouragingly. "I know you can do it. Listen, where are you staying?"

"At the bed-and-breakfast. I've booked a room there indefinitely."

Her brows lifted. "Oh wow. You really do expect this to take some time."

His face crumpled with worry. "I do. Farrah's one stubborn woman. It's why I married her, but it might also be the death of me."

"Well, do your best not to worry too much, but I know that's hard. In the meantime I'll try to talk some sense into her."

"Thank you."

She wrapped her arms around him and gave him a hug. When they parted, he glanced over toward Farrah, but her back was turned to them. He sighed before heading off into the crowd.

Ginny watched him go with a heavy heart. She was about to find Aiden and see where he'd gone off to when a woman walking toward her caught her attention.

"Why, if it isn't the Lighthouse Café owner."

Ellen was *the* real estate agent in town. She was also Aiden's ex-wife. She was a very fit and fabulous fiftyish blonde with platinum locks woven into the honey-colored ones. She had a thick coating of makeup, with dark eyeliner rimming her crystal-blue eyes, and leather pants hugged her legs. She wore a short black fur coat and diamond teardrop earrings.

"Ellen, how're you?"

"I'm great." She peered around Ginny. "You came alone? You and Aiden not a thing anymore?"

Ginny rolled her eyes. "We're still a thing."

"Oh," she replied, clearly disappointed. "Tell me, does Aiden still do that thing where he hugs you into his side while you walk?"

"I'm sorry?"

She shrugged. "It's just that my ex is so routine. He treats all his girl-friends the same way, does the same things with them—takes them on his boat, cooks them dinner. It all goes great until it falls apart. I hope that doesn't happen to you."

Ginny's jaw nearly dropped. Yes, Aiden had done all of those things with her—the boat and cooking. But the delighted sparkle in Ellen's eyes suggested that she was trying to get under Ginny's skin, and she wasn't about to let that happen.

"He's done those things—and more," she replied, lifting her eyebrows suggestively.

Ellen's mouth tightened. "Well, good luck, because it won't be long until all his sweetness dies and you'll be cast aside like the others. Good luck when that happens. I hope the heartbreak isn't too much."

An arm draped around Ginny's shoulder. Without looking, she knew it was Aiden. "Ellen, what brings you out and about at Christmas? Maxing out your credit cards?"

Ellen smirked. "I haven't done that in years. I'm only out getting a few gifts." She shot Ginny a saccharine smile. "Good seeing you again. Bye now."

As soon as she was gone, Aiden turned to her. "What was that all about?"

She didn't want to tell him how Ellen had acted because it would only anger him. "Oh, nothing. Just Ellen saying that she's glad we're doing well."

He scoffed. "That doesn't sound like her."

"That's because it's not." She sighed. Might as well tell him the truth. "She's not happy that we're together and she basically let me know."

"Well Ellen isn't part of my life now, and you are." He squeezed her tight. "Come on. Let's do some more shopping."

But even though Ginny knew her heart was supposed to lighten, it wouldn't. What Ellen had said put a sour taste in her mouth. She only hoped that taste would go away soon.

## Chapter Two

Farrah darted through the swinging door that led from the dining room of the restaurant into the kitchen. "Okay, I need five plates, three teas, and two waters. I'll get the drinks if you could take the plates out, Chandler and Reece. Thanks so much girls. They go to tables four and six."

She sailed past the women and began making drinks. Reece shot Ginny a look, and Chandler shook her head. Ever since Farrah had come to stay with them, she'd taken it upon herself to work in the café with gusto—too much gusto if you asked Ginny.

As Ginny finished plating chicken breasts smothered in a creamy sauce and garnished with mashed potatoes, Farrah sidled up to her. "I've been thinking about the Christmas week menu."

She quirked a brow. "You have?"

"Yes, and I was thinking that maybe we should tweak things a little bit. I know you want to make oyster dressing, but I was thinking we should do something a little more traditional. How about we do turkey and dressing with green bean casserole?"

"Farrah, I try to blend the local seafood into the dishes. That's what people like about my restaurant."

"I know, but since it's the holiday anyway, we could cut loose a little bit. Why don't you let me do the cooking that week, as a thank-you for letting me help you out and for letting me stay here?"

The worst thing would be to tell her best friend no, she couldn't help. So Ginny smiled. "I'll think about it. Oh, Chandler! Be sure to take the men at table six silverware. They don't have any."

Chandler paused as she headed toward the swinging door and nodded. "Will do."

Farrah tapped Ginny on the shoulder. "Well, I must be getting back to my tables. Duty calls."

She headed out and Reece came over. "Mama, when are you going to tell Aunt Farrah that she has to leave?"

"Shh. You'll hurt her feelings."

Her youngest daughter took the two plates that Ginny had built, one in each hand. "I love her the same as you, but my room isn't big enough for the two of us, even with Chandler staying with Hudson now."

Hudson was Chandler's fiancé. They'd be getting married after the first of the year on the beach. They were all looking forward to the ceremony, no one more so than Chandler.

And it was true what Reece said. Ever since Farrah had arrived with three overstuffed suitcases, it seemed like the room wasn't big enough. Clothes and knickknacks spilled out of the doorway into the hall. You could always tell where Farrah had been in the lighthouse because everywhere she went, a trail of clothes followed her.

Ginny sighed. "I know, but I can't kick her out, Reece. She's my best friend."

"And what about the Christmas menu? We've been working on it for weeks, making sure we get it right. Are you going to let her change it?"

"I don't know. If she wants to make an addition, that'll be okay."

"Really? It will be, when you've already worked to get the oysters and all the other ingredients? This is your first Christmas at the lighthouse. You want it to be special."

Her heart constricted just thinking that Farrah might take over her Christmas and change all the plans that she'd been working on for weeks. "Well, maybe with Brad being here, things will change."

"I doubt it. Farrah won't even talk to him."

Her daughter had a point. "Do me a favor," she told Reece. "Don't worry about any of this. It'll all work itself out. Things have a way of doing that, okay?"

"If you say so."

"I do say so."

Reece took the plates and left the kitchen. Ginny wiped her hands and headed into the dining room to check on the guests and make sure that everyone had what they needed.

When she opened the door, Farrah was signing for a package. The deliveryman nodded to Ginny before leaving, and she walked up to Farrah.

"Did you get something?"

Her best friend smiled. "Yes, we did get something. Come see."

They took the big box into the kitchen, and Farrah grabbed a knife and sliced into the tape. "I did a little poking around. Don't be mad at me, but with Christmas coming up, I had to make sure that we're fully stocked on supplies. When I noticed that the lighthouse is *less* than stocked, I took the liberty to purchase a few things to spruce up the place."

She opened the flaps to reveal an explosion of Christmas ornaments and decorations. There were yards of garland, ornaments, lights.

Ginny was speechless. "Wow. I don't know what to say."

Farrah winked. "You can thank me later, after we have this place all spruced up and ready to go. You know there's a contest in town, right?"

"Contest?"

"Uh-huh." She pulled out a package of garland and tore into it. "This'll be perfect."

"What were you saying about the contest?"

"Oh, right. There's a decorating contest for all the businesses. Don't worry, I've already entered you. The judging's not for a while."

"You what? Entered me into a contest?"

Farrah shot her a sympathetic look. "Now don't be angry. Not only will the contest expose you to new business, but it signifies that you're part of the community. That you belong in Sugar Cove."

"Farrah, I don't need a contest to prove that I'm part of this community."

"Of course you don't. But this will help either way. Now, don't worry about a thing. I'll handle all the decorating. You just focus on the cooking, except for the few days leading up to Christmas. I've got an entire new menu in mind."

Chandler poked her head into the box. "What's all this?"

"Decorations." Farrah lifted an ornament the size of a baseball. "Aren't they great. We're going to make this place look beautiful."

"They're great. We could use a little Christmas cheer."

Ginny silently shot Chandler a look that suggested she not encourage Farrah, but her daughter had already turned away.

Farrah continued sifting through the box. "I'm going to take care of everything. Now. Get back out there to your customers. Oh, but could you make me two sweet teas? Table one needs them."

For as much as she loved her best friend, Ginny felt the overwhelming urge to push Farrah right on out the front door and lock it so that she couldn't get back inside.

But it was wrong of her to feel that way. Her best friend needed her. But her best friend also needed to talk to Brad and sort out their marriage.

"Uncle Brad's here," Reece said, whizzing by.

Farrah dropped the ornament she held back into the box. "What does he want?"

"Wants to talk to you, I assume."

"Tell him to leave."

Ginny moved away and began making the teas. "You need to talk to him."

"There's nothing to say."

"You two haven't spoken since you arrived. Maybe there's an explanation."

Farrah shot her a scathing look. "What sort of explanation? He was having an affair."

"He's here to eat, and we can't simply ignore him."

"We can't?"

"Farrah," Ginny said in warning.

"You talk to him, then. I'll be here decorating."

Reece's eyes widened. "In the middle of lunch service?"

"Well, sure. You can't exactly expect me to be of any help when I'm emotionally traumatized, now can you?"

"No," Ginny mumbled. "I suppose we can't be."

She took the drinks to table one and spotted Brad sitting by himself at a table near the door. She walked over but wasn't sure if she should smile or not, so she nodded. "She's not coming out."

Brad rubbed a hand across his forehead. "I guess that would be asking too much."

"From the woman who won't even talk to you, yes, I think so."

He settled back in his chair and glanced around. "This is a nice place you have here, Ginny. You've done well. If the saying is make lemons into lemonade, then I'd say you've gone well beyond that."

"Thank you."

"What about the woman who lives in your old house?"

Savannah, the woman Ginny's dead husband had left their home to, had called Ginny a couple of weeks ago. For days Ginny had ignored the woman's calls, but when she'd finally answered the phone on Thanksgiving, it was the exact same time that Farrah had shown up and declared that Brad was cheating and that she had left him.

Since then, the calls had stopped and Ginny had put them out of her mind.

She slid onto the seat across from him. "That woman, Savannah," she said in reply to his question. "I have no idea how she's getting along, and frankly I don't care."

"I can understand that." They were silent for a long moment before Brad murmured, "She left when I was in the shower on Thanksgiving Day."

Ginny's eyes widened. "She didn't even tell you she was going? There wasn't an argument or anything?"

He raked his fingers through his hair. "No. She just left. She called me one time to say that she was fine and that she knew I was having an affair. But I swear to you that I'm not."

She folded her arms. For years her husband had been quietly cheating with Savannah. He'd even given her a son, and it had all happened under Ginny's nose. The only reason why she'd discovered any of it was because at the reading of Jack's will, he'd snatched the house away from her and given it to the other woman. So Ginny knew firsthand how well a person could be at hiding a life-changing secret from another, even someone they lived with.

"Then why does my best friend think that you're having an affair?"

He lifted his palms and shrugged. "I was planning a surprise party for our anniversary and she saw a text that got misconstrued. I've told her that it's not what she thinks it is, but she won't listen. I thought Farrah would leave for a few days, blow off some steam, and then come home. But you see how that's gone. Ginny"—he ripped his hand through his hair—"I'm a mess without her."

She believed him. Dark circles cupped the undersides of his eyes. His hair was disheveled, and his clothes were rumpled, looking like he'd pulled them straight from the suitcase and wiggled into them. This wasn't the Brad that Ginny knew. That Brad would never have left his house without his shirt pressed.

She looked over her shoulder as Farrah entered the dining room, took one look at Brad and whipped around on her heel before heading back into the kitchen.

Brad sighed and dropped his head into his hands. "She won't talk to me."

Ginny studied him for a moment. He looked beaten down, like he'd given up. She supposed the fact that his wife refused to talk to him was a huge contributor to that fact, so much so that she began to wonder if that was the whole problem. Brad wasn't *making* Farrah listen to him.

But either way, all she could do was offer advice, not live her friends' lives for them.

She rose and patted Brad's shoulder. "Don't worry. You'll get this all worked out."

"I hope so," was all he said as she walked away.

The rest of the lunch service went quickly. Brad ate and left, and before Ginny knew it, it was time to clean up.

"I'm beat," Reece said, slumping into a chair.

Ginny chuckled. "Don't sit down yet. We've got some cleaning to do."

She was about to lock the doors when she spotted a woman approaching to eat. Ginny opened the door and smiled. "I'm sorry, lunch is over."

A strong breeze snapped the woman's jacket open. She pulled it closed and lifted her head that was tucked into her chest to avoid the cold wind.

When she glanced up, Ginny's mouth dropped.

"Ginny?" the woman said.

Her blood became ice. "Savannah?"

"Do you have a minute to talk?"

No words came to her because here was the woman who had stolen her husband and her home. She stood outside of her house, and all Ginny could wonder was if this woman had arrived to steal the lighthouse from her, too.

## Chapter Three

"Please," Savannah said. "I won't take up much of your time."

She wanted to slam the door in the woman's face, to tell her to leave and never return. But Ginny was a Southern lady, and Southerners were kind almost to a fault.

"Yes, come in."

When she walked in, Reece's eyes became as big as plates. "Mama, what is she doing here?"

Reece, of course, knew who Savannah was because when she'd returned to their old house to visit, *that woman* had been the person who answered the door and told Reece that her mother was gone.

Ginny struggled to answer her daughter's question. "I don't know what she's doing here."

Savannah's gaze darted back and forth between them. "I'm not here to make trouble. I only wish to speak with you—alone."

Farrah entered from the kitchen with a strand of garland wrapped around her neck. "I thought I heard voices out here. Can I make a to-go plate?"

"No," Ginny said bitterly. "Farrah, this is Savannah."

It was a moment before her friend's jaw unhinged with the realization of exactly who this woman was.

Now all they were missing was Chandler. And then, right on cue, her oldest daughter walked in with her purse slung over her shoulder. "Oh, I didn't realize we had company."

"We don't," Ginny muttered. "This is Savannah. Savannah, this is my oldest daughter, Chandler."

Savannah didn't miss a beat. She smiled and nodded. "I have one son, but he's with my mother."

"Her son is y'alls half-brother."

Chandler ripped her gaze from Savannah and pinned it on her mother. "This is *that woman*?"

"This is her."

*That woman*, as they'd come to call Savannah, had the decency to turn a dark shade of red at the nickname. "I came to speak with you in private," she said.

"You're not looking to take anything else away from my best friend, are you?" Farrah said snidely. "As far as I'm concerned, you've already taken enough."

Her head dropped to her chest. "I know there's nothing that I can say that'll change how y'all feel about me."

"You're right," Farrah replied in a steely voice, "there isn't."

Savannah had called Ginny nonstop for weeks, and now she was standing in her home. The least she could do was offer her a cup of coffee and hear her out.

She shooed her daughters and friend away. "Can y'all give us a few minutes?"

"Sure," Reece said, shooting Farrah a poisonous look. "I'm going for a run anyway."

"And I'm spending the afternoon with Hudson's sister," Chandler added. "She's in town and wants to help with the wedding."

"I've got nowhere to be," Farrah said dryly. "But I'll gladly give you some space. But only for a few minutes," she said pointedly to Savannah. "You're not allowed to hurt my best friend anymore. Haven't you done enough?"

Savannah didn't answer, and Ginny hadn't expected her to. But one by one the women left, leaving the two rivals alone.

She pointed to a table. "Can I get you some coffee?"

Savannah uncurled her fingers from the purse she held. "That would be nice. I drove pretty much straight here, only stopping for bathroom breaks."

Ginny moved off, calling over her shoulder. "How'd you find me?"

She heard the scraping of chair feet against the floor as Savannah pulled a chair out and sat. "I asked around. After you wouldn't take my calls, I found some of your old friends and hounded them until they told me where you'd gone."

She hounded her old friends, huh? The only true old friend that Ginny had was Farrah. The others had been rich, viperous women jumping on just about any and all gossip that they could get their ears around.

She poured Savannah a cup of coffee and loaded it on a tray with milk and a pot of sugar. When she returned to the dining room, Savannah had her jacket off and she sat at the table, hands folded so hard that her knuckles were white hills.

"Thank you," the woman said as she took the cup of coffee and poured milk and much more sugar into it than Ginny thought was healthy for a person.

"You're welcome."

She sat and eyed Savannah, wondering if it had been the right choice to invite her into her home, but it wasn't as if the woman were a vampire and being invited in was the only way that she could attack her, now was it?

For some reason Ginny wasn't so sure if Savannah wasn't secretly a vampire, one who fed on married men.

The mistress cleared her throat. "I know you didn't answer when I called you, and I can understand why, after what happened with the house."

"You mean when my husband willed it to you and pulled the rug out from under me? Or the part when I only had an hour to vacate the premises and the house became yours?"

Heat bloomed on *that woman's* cheeks. "Honestly I didn't know about any of that. I didn't know that Jack would leave the house to me. I didn't think I'd get much of anything, to be honest."

She wasn't sure she believed any of that. "But you did know that when you got together with my husband, he was already married."

Her blush deepened. "Yes, I knew that."

"And it didn't stop you from sleeping with him and having unprotected sex."

Which, now that Ginny thought about it, that had exposed her to goodness knew what kind of diseases. Thank goodness Jack hadn't given her anything.

"It also didn't stop you from having his child," Ginny said, unable to stop herself.

She'd dreamed about what she would say to Savannah if they were ever face-to-face, and no, she wasn't at a loss for words. This woman deserved every bit of ire that Ginny had to throw.

"But I also know," she added, "that it takes two to tango, and that Jack was just as guilty as you, even more so, because he turned his back on our marriage vows. He kept you and your son a secret, and that must've been hard for you, not having a husband who could claim you and his son outright."

Savannah nodded slightly.

"And I've also heard that the women in Buckhead haven't been terribly kind given that you took over my house and my life."

A tear welled in Savannah's eye. She knuckled it away before it spilled onto her cheek, and took a staggered breath. "No, they haven't been kind. No one's welcomed me with open arms. I have a house and some money, but money doesn't buy happiness."

"Tell me about it," Ginny muttered.

Jack had become wealthy while they'd been married, and even though they didn't want for anything, he'd still kept a tight leash on spending, and hadn't given Ginny free rein to buy herself new clothes whenever she wanted them. In fact, he'd been somewhat of a miser. That was why when he'd passed away, Ginny had finally felt like she would have a chance to gain a tiny grain of freedom with their money. She wouldn't be scolded for making an extravagant purchase or two. But that had been snatched away when she was given only a fraction of Jack's wealth and had been forced from their home—*her* home.

Savannah sipped her coffee and placed the cup on top of the table with a quiet thud. "No, things haven't been great for me. I thought that once I had the house, that my life would be wonderful, but I've realized that it's not. I want to move back home, to South Carolina."

Ginny drummed her fingers on top of the table. "And your son?"

"Jack was never around much to begin with, so they were never really given the chance to bond like a dad who was present all the time would have with his child."

Ginny almost said that she was sorry but stopped herself. Savannah had made her bed in life, and now it was time for her to lay in it.

"Well, your experience with Jack isn't much different from how it was when my girls were young. He wasn't home much. He worked a lot. So I had to do most of the raising."

She nodded. "It seems that not much changed between then and now."

No, a lot had changed. Jack was dead and he'd stolen her life. Ginny had worked hard to keep the bitterness of his actions from consuming her, and she thought that she'd done a great job, but with Savannah here now, she wasn't so sure.

"What is it that you came here for?" she asked, feeling like this conversation was an emotional roller coaster that she wanted to jump off of.

Savannah swallowed hard. "To be honest, I'm here because I'm not happy with the house. I'm not happy with Atlanta, and I want to offer you a chance to have your life back."

It felt like someone had just plucked one of her heartstrings. Her whole body snapped to attention. "What do you mean, offer me my life back?"

Savannah exhaled a deep breath and tucked her hair behind both ears. She looked up at Savannah with her blue eyes shining and said in a trembling voice, "I called you all those times to say that you can have your house. You can move back to Atlanta and have everything that Jack—and I—took from you."

## Chapter Four

"She said what, that she would give it to you?"

Ginny bent over and picked up a seashell that was half-buried in the sand. The water lapped at her ankles as she retrieved the clam from the beach.

"No," she told Aiden, who had folded the bottom of his khaki pants to his ankles. "She's not going to give it to me. She'll sell it, though, and at half the cost of what she would normally get."

"Wow." He slid his hands into his pockets. "That's being mighty generous."

"Is it?" She brushed hair away from her mouth. "Or is it guilt that's making her do this?"

He pressed his thumb and forefinger together. "Maybe a teensy bit of guilt."

She laughed. "Maybe a lot of guilt."

"Probably so. But maybe she's doing it because she feels like it's the right thing to do."

Ginny sighed as she kept walking along the beach. "Is it the right thing? It sounded to me like she'll sell it because she doesn't fit in."

"But she could get more for it." He gently nudged her elbow with his. "That should mean something."

"It should," she agreed.

The sun was setting on the horizon, smearing brilliant colors across the sky—cotton candy, blue raspberry and creamsicle. She inhaled the briny air and dropped her shoulders, letting the tension fall away.

Ever since Savannah had appeared earlier in the day and made her offering, Ginny had been tied up in knots.

"What are you going to do?"

"Honestly?"

"Honestly."

She stopped and stared into his blue eyes. "I don't know. First, I never considered that this would be offered to me. When I arrived in Sugar Cove, I didn't know who I was, and I barely had a plan for my life. But now I feel like I'm settled. Things are good. But Aiden, I spent a life in Atlanta, building it, making connections. Farrah's my best friend, but there are still others."

"Well, sure. I can understand that. You lived most of your life there. But can you return to that house, knowing what you know about Jack?"

She smirked. "You wouldn't have an ulterior motive for getting me to stay, would you?"

He smiled. "If I did, would that be so bad?"

"No, of course not. But you've got a point. What would living in that house be like, knowing that Jack had stolen it out from under me. Not only that, but that our life had been a lie."

"Not a lie," he argued. "Just maybe not what you thought it was."

She hugged her arms. He was right. Her life with Jack hadn't been what she believed. It had been full of an underlying betrayal. How could she return to her house knowing that? But at the same time, she missed things about her old life.

"I guess it's something that I'm going to have to think about," she told him.

"I guess so," he said kindly, but Ginny heard the sorrow in his voice and knew that if she left Sugar Cove, that her relationship with Aiden would be over.

*  *  *

"I'm going shopping for Christmas decorations," Farrah announced the next morning, "and Ginny, you're coming with me."

"I am?"

She'd planned to spend the day reading and catching up on some cleaning, but when Farrah whisked into her room with her purse slung over her shoulder, Ginny knew her plans were about to change.

Farrah tugged her from the chair. "Yes, you are. We need more decor if we're going to have the café in tip-top shape by the time Christmas arrives. There are only a few things that we need, but they're important. So come on."

There was no point in complaining because when Farrah wanted something, she got it.

So without one peep of grumbling, Ginny pulled on her jacket and grabbed her purse before heading out with her best friend.

Besides, this would give her the perfect opportunity to find out exactly what evidence Farrah had against Brad.

It was cloudy when they headed outside. There was a slight chill in the air, so Ginny zipped her jacket to her throat.

"Where are we going?" she asked.

"One of those little pop-up Christmas stores opened in downtown Port St. Joe. I thought we'd head there and then grab some lunch." She glanced over her shoulder to Ginny as she headed to her car. "You know, just some girl time. You spend all your days so busy with the café that I figured a little one-on-one would do you good."

Ginny wasn't going to argue about that.

The drive to Port St. Joe only took a few minutes, and by the time they arrived, it was midmorning and all the sidewalks were filled with shoppers.

"I guess we weren't the only ones with this idea," Farrah noted.

"I guess not."

They parked and headed out. A food truck selling hot drinks was their first stop. Farrah grabbed a white chocolate mocha and Ginny took a hot apple cider. Nothing beat cider on a cold day.

"I talked to Brad," she told Farrah.

She lifted a brow. "Oh? And what did the cheater say?"

"That he didn't cheat."

"Oh, look at these beautiful ornaments." She dragged her fingers over a golden star. "Aren't they gorgeous? This would look beautiful on the tree I'm decorating for you."

"You're decorating a tree?"

"Of course. One is on the way thanks to a certain online shopping store. Don't look at me like that. Buying you a tree is the least I can do to thank you for taking me in."

"Speaking of that"—Ginny took the bundle of ornaments that Farrah dropped in her hands—"what about Brad?"

"What about him?"

"He's upset. Really upset, and I don't think you're being fair to him."

Farrah stopped inspecting a particularly jovial porcelain Santa and fixed her stare on Ginny. "You don't think I'm being fair when I found a series of texts from someone named S, and what S said to Brad is that last time had been great, and that S couldn't wait to meet up again?"

Ginny was hit with a bolt of lightning. That text seemed to contradict what Brad had told her about putting together a party for Farrah. She had to admit that it sounded bad. But she'd never known Brad to lie before.

"But cheating just doesn't seem like him," she argued. "He loves you."

"Well, he's off having an amazing time with S, so you be the judge of that."

Farrah slipped down an aisle that seemed to have suffered from a ribbon explosion. Ginny followed. "But still, you have to talk to him. You can't just ignore your husband."

"Why can't I?"

She laughed uneasily. "Because you have to discuss about things. Are you going to see a counselor?"

"Why should I?" She rubbed a red and white striped ribbon between two fingers. "It seems that Brad's made up his mind about what he wants out of this relationship. I should have, too."

"And what is it that you want?"

"I think this ribbon will look good on the tree, don't you?" When Ginny didn't answer, Farrah plucked it from the display table. "Let's see what else they've got."

"Farrah, you're avoiding the question."

"I'm not avoiding it; I'm just choosing not to answer. There's a difference."

She rolled her eyes. There wasn't a difference to her. "Fine. If you don't want to tell me, at least tell your husband so that he's not being tormented."

"Why shouldn't I torment him? He's tormented me."

Ginny shook her head, not believing what her friend was saying. "First of all, because that's not fair. He's been a good husband, at least up until now."

Farrah just shrugged. Even though the evidence sounded bad, Ginny wasn't convinced that Brad was cheating. "I wish you'd sit down with him and talk it out."

"I will. When I'm ready. And right now I'm not ready. Oh, look at those cute little climbing Santas." Farrah dragged her to a corner of the store where a small Santa was climbing a ladder that leaned against a tree. Her best friend glanced at the price tag. "A little out of my budget. Oh well, maybe next year."

As they continued shopping, all Ginny could be was sad that her best friend's marriage of over twenty years was over, and surprised that Farrah didn't seem to care. This wasn't like her best friend. Normally Farrah would be crying and upset about news like this. But she was acting like her husband cheating was no big deal. It didn't make any sense.

Farrah dropped one last ornament into the basket she carried and whipped around, a wide smile on her face. "Looks like that's it. Ready to check out?"

"Sure."

They reached the counter, and Farrah painstakingly placed every ornament and spool of ribbon atop the surface for the cashier to ring up.

A woman with curly dark hair whizzed by. She was lean and wore lots of gold jewelry—bangles and rings, necklaces and loopy earrings.

She spotted the two women and smiled widely. "Thank y'all for coming in. Is this your first time?"

"It sure is, but I have a feeling it won't be our last," Farrah said with a wink.

The woman laughed lightly. "I'm so glad you enjoyed it. Are y'all from around here?"

"Well she"—Farrah pointed to Ginny—"lives in Sugar Cove and I'm just visiting."

*With no plans to leave,* Ginny thought.

"Oh?" The woman turned her attention to Ginny. "You're not visiting?"

"No, I own the Lighthouse Café."

The woman's eyes widened briefly before her gaze dropped to the ornaments that were carefully being packaged by the cashier. "The café? The one that's in the old lighthouse?"

"The one and only."

"Oh, um, that's interesting. Well, I hope y'all have a great day shopping."

Without another word the woman raced off as if she couldn't get away from them fast enough.

Ginny and Farrah exchanged a look. That was strange. Usually when she told someone that she owned the café, they gushed about how they heard the food was so good and they were dying to try it but hadn't made it there yet.

But why was this woman acting like Ginny was on fire or something?

As the cashier gave Farrah the total and her friend paid, her gaze drifted back to the store owner. She stood huddled in the corner talking to another woman. Ginny explicitly spotted the woman glancing in her direction, and the second woman looked, too. When the owner realized that Ginny had seen them, her face turned a deep shade of red and she turned away.

Okay, that could have meant anything, but to Ginny, when two people both looked up at one person, that meant they were talking about said person. Why were they talking about her? And stranger of all, why had they looked guilty? What was going on?

Farrah paid and Ginny helped her with the bags. As they left the store, Ginny told her what she'd seen.

"Yes, I agree, that woman acted strangely," Farrah said.

"But why? I've never met her before."

"Don't look so worried. I'm sure it's nothing. Come on. Let's put these bags in the trunk and go have some lunch. What do you say?"

"Sure," she said half-heartedly.

They stowed the bags, and as they walked to find something to eat, Ginny couldn't shake the feeling that those women hadn't only been talking about her, whatever it was they were gossiping about, it was bad. Very bad.

She just hoped it wasn't so bad that whatever it was couldn't be overcome.

## Chapter Five

As soon as they returned to the house, Farrah collected all the Christmas decorations and placed them in the dining room. She got her Bluetooth speaker up and running, and within minutes the sound of Carrie Underwood singing carols was filling the lighthouse.

Ginny had just relaxed into her bedroom, hoping to read the book that she'd started, when Farrah's head popped in. "Ready to help me decorate?"

"Oh, we're decorating?"

"Of course, silly. Why else did we bother to go shopping? I've got everything organized. All we need to do is get it up. It'll only take a few minutes."

"A few minutes?" she asked skeptically.

Whenever her friend said that something would take a few minutes, that usually meant a few days. But how many decorations did they have? Probably not very many, so it couldn't take too long.

"I'll get Reece to help us, too. You'll see. We'll be done in no time."

Farrah left her room, calling for Reece. Several minutes later the three of them stood in the dining room, which looked like a Christmas explosion.

There were wreaths and lights, boughs of green dotted with red berries, golden ornaments the size of softballs, and lots of glass deer.

"Where did you get all of this?" Ginny asked in shock.

"Oh, here and there. I've been buying for a while." She smiled at them. "Now, let's put the tree together and decorate."

Twenty minutes later Ginny was still holding the same strand of garland that she'd picked up fifteen minutes earlier.

"Now where do you think I should put this ornament?" Farrah asked, holding it up to the tree.

For every single ornament it had been the same question, where should it go?

"Why don't you just let us put them on?" Reece asked, yawning.

"I want to make sure that they're put up perfectly," Farrah replied, holding the orb and stepping back to study the tree that only had ten ornaments on it. "I'd like for it to be symmetrical, and often having others watch is a good way to make sure that happens."

"Aunt Farrah, usually we just put the ornaments on and don't worry about it."

"I'm not worried," she added quickly. "I just want to make sure it's perfect."

"Oh, it's perfect all right."

"Ginny?" she asked. "Where do you think it should be?"

"Wherever you'd like."

At this rate they wouldn't be finished decorating until tomorrow, and Ginny had a date with Aiden later that night to walk through the Tinsel Trail.

Reece slumped into a chair and sighed. "Since we're here, have you decided what you're going to do about the house?"

Ginny cringed. "I don't know."

"Well, you can't leave Sugar Cove," Farrah said, startled. "This is your home now. You can't just go back."

"But that was my home for a long time, too."

Panic filled Farrah's eyes. "But what about your business and your new life?"

"I like the beach," Reece added. "Don't get me wrong. I love Atlanta, too. But the pace is so much slower here. It's so calm. My blood pressure's good now."

Ginny tossed back her head and laughed. "You're in your twenties. You don't have to worry about your blood pressure."

"I know. But someday I will." She jerked her head toward Farrah, who was still eyeing the tree and figuring out where to place the ornament. "And it looks like it'll be sooner rather than later."

"But honestly, Ginny. You love living here. Why would you leave?"

Ginny folded her arms. "Are you worried that if I go, you won't have a place to hide from Brad?"

"No, of course not." Farrah sniffed. Enough about Brad. We'll talk when I'm good and ready, and him showing up on your doorstep isn't going to make that happen any sooner." She turned back to the tree. "Now, where exactly should I put this?"

"I don't know, but I've got a date with Ted tonight, and unless I start getting ready soon, I'm going to be late."

Which reminded Ginny. "And I've got one with Aiden."

Farrah frowned. "Oh, so I'll be all alone."

"You could call—"

"Don't you say Brad," her friend replied.

"Brad," Ginny told her with a raised eyebrow.

She smirked. "I'd rather have a date with a Christmas tree."

Well, it looked like that was what Farrah was going to get, whether she liked it or not.

* * *

"It was really strange," Ginny told Aiden. "I didn't understand why they were gossiping about me. Do I have the sort of face that begs people to gossip?"

They wove their way through the park that was dotted with Christmas trees, all decorated and sponsored by local businesses.

He shrugged. "Maybe they were just jealous of your flourishing business."

"Oh yeah, maybe that was it," she said sarcastically.

"You never know." He stopped and faced her. "Are you sure that you want to spend our walk through the Tinsel Trail talking about people you don't know personally?"

She sighed. "No, of course not. But it was really strange. I mean, I just didn't get it because it was obvious that they were talking about me."

He placed a hand on her shoulder and kneaded some of the tension out. "I don't think you should be worried about it."

"And I have a feeling that I should be."

They stopped at a tree topped with a cutout of the Grinch's head. The whole thing was decorated in lime green and red.

Aiden frowned. "I'm not sure if I should be traumatized by this tree or intrigued."

She laughed and nudged his stomach with her elbow. "I think you should be wowed at someone's creativity."

"I think you're right." He slipped a hand over her shoulder. "But I'm still not finished with this conversation. Why're you so worried about what other people think or say? You've got a thriving business. You're doing great."

She looked up and smiled at him. "I know, it's just that I guess with Farrah being here, everything's been a little more stressful than normal. I'm off my routine. I love my best friend, I do."

"Of course you do."

"But she's a little under someone's foot."

"You mean yours?"

"That's the one."

He lifted his head back and laughed, which made the corners of his eyes crinkle in a way that warmed her heart. When his laughter died down, Aiden gave her a sincere smile. "Have you tried talking to her?"

"And saying, what? You're driving me crazy. Can you please find someplace else to live?"

"No, not like that. Of course not. You know, I used to have a buddy when I was young who had gone through a rough breakup, a divorce actually. I wasn't married yet, so I was still living alone."

"Living the bachelor life," she teased.

He smoothed a hand over his head nervously as if he was afraid to admit it. Ginny elbowed him playfully. "It's okay. I know you had a life before I entered and turned it upside down," she joked.

He stared at her for a long moment. The breeze picked up and blew a few strands of hair into her face. Aiden gently lifted them where they'd plastered themselves to her mouth and tucked them behind her ear. "And what if I told you that you have turned my world upside down?"

"Well"—she swallowed past a knot in her throat and watched as his gaze trailed down her neck—"I suppose that I'd say, in some ways you've done the same to me. I never expected to meet anyone like you, Aiden."

"And I never expected to meet anyone like you, either."

The air around them tightened with tension, and Ginny was acutely aware of how he looked at her with tenderness, how the tops of her cheeks were warming, and how it felt like she was falling into his eyes.

But they were at a Tinsel Tree walk, not all alone, so she cleared her throat. "You were telling me about your friend."

"That's right." He ripped his gaze from her and steered them back down the path. "He was my best friend, so of course I didn't care if he crashed on my couch for a while."

"But," she teased. "I hear a *but* coming."

"Yeah, there's a but." They wound their way around a tree decorated with oyster shells. "After about six months he was still sleeping on my couch, which was fine, but he also started rearranging things in my home, making it into his place more than it was mine."

"What would he do?"

"Moved the living room furniture around, placed the TV in the wrong spot."

She laughed. "What a sin that must've been."

He smirked. "What can I say, I like my TV a certain way."

"So is that all he did?"

"No, that wasn't all. He was using my place as a crutch so that he didn't have to move on with his life." Aiden sighed and sank onto one hip. "That was the hardest part to watch."

"So what'd you do?"

"I tried talking to him about it, but it didn't work. He'd deny that was what he was doing. But I was his friend."

"So you knew better."

"Right."

They wove through the crowd as people oohed and aahed at the trees. At first Ginny had been worried that Christmas at the beach wouldn't feel like Christmas, but she'd been wrong. The spirit of giving and love was everywhere, and it filled her heart with joy.

But her conversation with Aiden wasn't over. "So what did you do about your friend?"

"You mean to help him figure out that it was time for him to pick up the pieces of his own life?"

"Right."

"I'm not happy to say it."

"What is it?" she asked with an elbow nudge.

"I made it annoying for him to live with me."

She laughed. "You didn't."

"I'm ashamed to admit it, but that's true."

A line of people walked right toward them, and Aiden steered Ginny out of their path protectively. It occurred to her that Jack, if he'd still been alive, never would've done that for her. She glanced up shyly at Aiden, who looked down at her and smiled.

She quickly glanced away, returning to the story. "So what did you do to annoy him?"

"Mind you, this is after I tried talking to him and telling him that it was time for him to get back to his life."

"So that didn't go well."

"No, it didn't. He said that he was perfectly happy to stay with me, at my house."

"You've got magnetism," she joked.

"I've got something." He slipped his hands into his pockets as they stopped to admire a tree decorated by the fire department. Santas dressed up as firemen climbed little ladders that hung from nearly every bow. "So when talking to him didn't help, I had to go in a different direction."

"What direction was that?"

He shrugged. "The direction where I played music late at night, left dirty dishes piled up, stopped taking out the trash. That sort of stuff."

She chuckled. "So you basically turned into a frat boy."

"Something like that." His gaze slid to the corner of his eye as he watched her. "But you're not asking the most important question."

"Which is?"

"Did it work?"

"Okay, you're right. I forgot all about that. So did it, great leader, work?"

He smirked. "Remind me never to tell you my deep dark secrets."

"What? Afraid I'll laugh at them?"

"Yes."

She grinned. "I won't. Trust me. So, did it work? Did your friend leave?"

He swung his arm over her shoulder and pulled her into his side. "Let me just say this—he quickly discovered that he missed out on the world, and that my home was too small for the both of us."

"And are you still friends?"

"Of course. I know how to keep friends. That's what I'm saying. You can keep Farrah as your friend. But if you feel like she's hiding from something, sometimes people need a little nudge so that they get out there and live their lives."

She thought about that for a moment. Perhaps Farrah did need a nudge. Maybe that's just what Ginny would do.

## Chapter Six

But it turned out that nudging Farrah was harder than Ginny thought it would be. She left dirty dishes piled up, but Farrah washed them. When she turned the TV up too loud, Farrah very nicely asked her to lower it.

When Ginny let the trash stack up, Farrah emptied it. It seemed like there was no way to irk her friend enough to get Farrah to want to leave.

And when the café wasn't open, Farrah was spending all her free time buying decorations and putting them up.

"We're going to win the decorating contest," she announced early Monday morning. Her hands were on her hips, and she surveyed the explosion of Christmas proudly. "The judging's coming up. We'll be at the top of the list, surely."

If they weren't, Ginny figured the judges hated the holiday season. Farrah had spent every minute of her time wrapping lights around poles, strewing garland across surfaces, hanging ornaments in places where Ginny never thought to see an ornament. There were so many tiny Christmas lights that when they were turned on, Ginny had to lower the thermostat to ease the heat flaring in her body.

"If we don't win, I'd say the contest is rigged," Reece said as she wiped down tables.

"I'd have to agree with you," Farrah said, taking the cloth that Reece handed her and cleaning a surface.

The front door opened, and Chandler stepped in, stopping and staring at the decorations. She released a low whistle. "What happened in here?"

"I've been decorating. What do you think?"

"I think it's..." Her gaze landed on Ginny, who jerked her head toward Farrah as if to silently suggest that whatever Chandler had to say, it needed to be positive. "I think it looks great. Really wonderful. It's like I've stepped inside the North Pole."

Farrah clapped her hands with joy. "That's what I was hoping for. That you've walked into the North Pole. Looks like my goal is accomplished. Now I just have to make sure that we win."

"There are no guarantees on that," Ginny pointed out. "But you've done your best here, and that's what's important."

Just then the door opened and their first customer of the day arrived. Since it was Monday, that usually meant that they would be flooded with diners, so Ginny greeted the couple and quickly found a table for them.

She served them that day's meal—meatloaf and mashed potatoes—and then readied for the wave of folks who would enter the restaurant.

But the wave never came. Diners only trickled in, a fraction of their usual number of guests. It was strange, but everyone had an off day now and then, didn't they?

She tried not to be bothered by it as they finished up both lunch services and it was time to clean. Instead of worrying about things that she couldn't control, Ginny threw herself into working on the next day's meal, making sure that it was the best that it could be for the patrons who would come on Tuesday, because Tuesday would be better.

But on Tuesday even less people came. Had a new restaurant opened? Were they taking all of Ginny's regulars away? But when she asked around, no one had heard of a new dining establishment. So Ginny tucked her worry away and focused on Wednesday.

But it turned out to be the same as the two days prior. In fact, it was worse. As much as she didn't want to worry, and as much as she told herself not to, she couldn't help but to be saddled with doubt. What was going on? Why was her business drying up?

It didn't make any sense. But Ginny told herself not to worry. She wouldn't do that; so she swallowed down the knot in her throat and kept on cooking.

But by the time Friday rolled around and only a few people trickled in for lunch, Ginny knew that something was terribly, terribly wrong.

She worried that if she didn't do something about the lack of customers, she'd have to shut her doors sooner rather than later. In fact, with the expenses of payroll and buying supplies, her bank account was already quickly drying up. If business kept heading in this trajectory, then it wouldn't be long before her café was belly up and she'd have no choice but to take Savannah up on her offer to buy back her house and return to her old life in Atlanta.

But as much as she thought that idea would appeal to her, all it did was make a harder knot coil in her stomach.

Ginny loved her life in Sugar Cove, but it was quickly slipping away. If she didn't find out why, and soon, it would all be gone with a snap of her fingers.

## Chapter Seven

### FARRAH

Farrah didn't understand what was going on with the Lighthouse Café, but she was determined to find out. She'd decorated the place to the hilt. The food was fabulous. The restaurant was in a convenient location. So why was business drying up?

It just didn't make sense.

She'd told Ginny that she was going out to get some supplies. Her best friend in all the world had wanted to go, but Farrah had convinced her to stay in the house. She looked awful. It was obvious that worry was gnawing away at her. Dark circles were cupping the undersides of her eyes, and she hadn't been eating.

Whatever was going on, it angered Farrah. Ginny had worked so hard to make sure that her new life was successful, and now it was being shattered.

Farrah arrived in Port St. Joe and parked in an open spot downtown. Were these restaurants slow? Had the economy taken a turn for the worst?

She peeked into store windows and studied the amount of people trickling inside the local pizza joint. But in this town there was no sign that a recession was looming, or even hanging above anyone's head like a rain cloud. The businesses were busy. So what was going on with the café?

Farrah smelled a rat, and she didn't like the scent of decay.

She was about to head to the grocery store when a familiar voice stopped her.

"Farrah."

Pinpricks danced their way up her spine at the sound of Brad's voice. Darn. She'd worked so hard to avoid him, and he'd managed to track her down anyway.

"Brad," she said flatly as he stalked down the sidewalk, beelining straight for her.

She folded her arms and took a defensive stance. No matter what that man had to say, nothing was going to change her mind about what she'd seen.

He stopped in front of her and smiled down. "Fancy meeting up with you like this."

"Can it, Brad. You've probably been following me."

His cheeks turned a dark shade of plum. "Not following."

"Just spying casually? Is that it?"

"Is it so bad if I want to speak with my wife?" He sighed heavily. "You're not answering my calls."

"For good reason."

"It's not a good reason," he huffed. Realizing he was allowing his temper to get the better of him, Brad closed his eyes and pinched the bridge of his nose. "Can we please just talk? Over lunch? Someplace public. *Please.*"

Her heart lurched then, and it was a feeling that she didn't like. The truth was, she had been avoiding him, and whichever way their relationship went, at some point Farrah would have to discuss their future. She'd have to sit down and hash things out with Brad.

Better sooner than later.

She motioned toward the closest restaurant. "After you."

Brad didn't go first. He was a Southern gentleman, and that meant that he walked alongside Farrah as they moseyed inside the busy American-style restaurant.

"This is a nice little town," he murmured.

"Oh?" She curled a brow. "Getting to know the locals, are you?"

"Would you stop? I'm not getting to know anyone, Farrah. I've been pacing the floors of my room at the bed-and-breakfast, calling you and watching television. I don't know anybody down here, and the one person I do know won't talk to me."

He lowered his voice as the hostess asked how many in their party and seated them at a table that overlooked downtown.

"Nice view," Farrah murmured. "Of the street," she clarified, not wanting Brad to think that she was talking about him.

He sat and she read the menu—or tried to. Her skin was buzzing with nerves being this close to Brad. She wished he'd just give up and go home. They could talk about things after Christmas, once the holidays were over.

"I don't have much appetite," he murmured.

She didn't comment. She didn't have one, either, but she wasn't going to let him know that. So when the waiter arrived, Farrah ordered a double cheeseburger and fries.

Brad ordered a salad.

When the waiter left, she sat back in her chair and exhaled, studying the face of the man she'd loved for twenty-five years. Every line, wrinkle, she'd watched them form. She'd seen them wedge their way into his skin. She knew what most of them were from—worrying about their children, wondering if there was enough money to make it to the end of the month (when they were young and first starting out), caring for his mother when she got sick with dementia.

Yes, Farrah knew those lines, and she also spotted the new tiny fissure in his forehead that had been caused by the stress of her leaving.

"Farrah, how long do you plan to keep this up?" he asked as if she were a petulant child and not a grown woman.

"Keep this up?" she scoffed. "What exactly am I keeping up, Brad?"

He waved his hand dismissively. "This whole charade. Listen, I know what you think you read."

"I know what I saw." She tapped a finger hard on the table. Her nails were short now, thanks to working at the café. The acrylic didn't clack against the slick top like it normally would have. "That text said that whoever she was, she was looking forward to next time. Don't think I'm some dumb twenty-year-old who can be swayed by lies."

He rubbed a hand down his face. "Farrah, I didn't want to tell you this, but that was about a surprise party—for you. For our anniversary. I was trying to do something nice. I was meeting with a party planner. I can't help it that she said something about looking forward to next time, and let me be clear—when she said that, she meant the next time we were going to meet up to talk about the party. There wasn't anything else going on."

"Huh," was all she said.

"Look." He unwrapped his straw and dropped it into the glass of tea in front of him. Then he twisted the paper around his fingers while he spoke. "I know that I'm not a perfect husband. No one is. But I've done everything that I can to make our lives the best they can possibly be. I haven't been perfect—"

"You can say that again."

Anger flashed bright and hot in his eyes when he glanced up at her. He sighed and his chest deflated. "I deserved that. I'll take the hit. But what happened between us"—he dropped his voice and leaned over the table—"that was years ago. Haven't I earned your trust since then?"

Had he? She supposed so. Brad hadn't slipped in years. He hadn't done anything stupid in forever.

"That was one time, Farrah. One time, and I've worked myself to death trying to make it up to you. Don't I get a little grace, a little trust?"

She sat back and studied him as the waiter arrived with their food. When her basket filled with fries and the cheeseburger was settled in front of her, Farrah suddenly lost her appetite.

Brad picked up his fork and started eating. "You want to know what I think?"

"What could you possibly think?"

He shot her a scathing look. "I think you want a reason to hold this against me. You never forgave me for the past, so now you're wanting to tie me up and accuse me of something that hasn't even happened so that you can finally get back at me. Look, Farrah, I didn't have to tell you about that one time, but I did because I love you and you deserved to know."

"No, Brad, you didn't tell me because of that. You told me because I found her panties. End of story."

Her stomach clenched at the memory of those red lace panties tucked into her husband's underwear drawer. What a moron. Who left the evidence of their affair in plain sight for everyone to see?

"That was five years ago," he reminded her.

Five years of holding on to the pain, of counseling with their preacher and doing everything that she could to forgive him. The shame of it had been so unbearable that Farrah hadn't even told her best friend. Ginny didn't know. It also would've been the right time to tell her when she found out about what Jack had done to her friend, but even then Farrah had secreted this knowledge away, locking it in her heart so that no one would know her shame.

"Can't you ever find it in your heart to forgive me?" he asked.

She chewed on a French fry a long time before finally saying, "Once trust is broken like that, it takes a long time for it to come back, if it ever does. I could choose right now to trust you, but what if you're lying about that text? I'd be a fool to let myself fall into a trap like that. Fool me once, shame on you. Fool me twice, shame on me. That's the saying, and it's true. I've let you fool me once, and I took you back. But I can't let myself go through that kind of pain again."

Her heart had almost broken completely in two after she'd uncovered Brad's affair. For her to experience that a second time would be unbearable. So it was best to cut things off at the knees, end the relationship now, when she still had so much more life to live.

"And what about the kids, Farrah?" he asked, his eyes squinting as he tried to puzzle out how exactly to go about their lives. "What am I supposed to tell them?"

"The truth. That I've left you because you weren't faithful."

He slumped back into the chair and rubbed his mouth. "I'm not telling them that."

"They're out of college. They're grown-up. We all have to admit our mistakes at one point or another. There's no time like the present, don't you think?"

He shook his head sadly. "You know, you used to be reasonable. You used to listen. I've admitted my mistakes, Farrah. But what have you admitted here? That you don't have any room in your heart to listen to a man who's telling you the truth. That's what. Never did I think that I'd see the day when you'd turn your back on me, on your family."

"I'm not turning my back on anyone," she hissed. "You stopped caring about this family when you did your little dance a few years ago. I've tried, Brad. I've tried for five years, and seeing that text is what's convinced me that even after all this time, I still don't trust you. I don't.

What do you want me to do about that? Live a life where I'm reading everything that comes into your phone because I'm not sure if you're lying to me or not? No. I refuse for things to be that way. I want a life built on trust. Not worry and sadness, and that's what's been going on for years. I'm sick of it."

The anger that fueled her speech surprised even Farrah. Where had it come from? It came from her soul, from the small pit inside of her that had grown and grown, mistrust and fear curling up into a knot that had festered until it was ready to be spewed out in that moment.

"I'm not hungry anymore." She dropped her napkin on the basket and shoved back her chair. "You can stop trying to talk to me. There's no point. Now if you'll excuse me."

She rose and started to walk past him when Brad's hand shot out and took her wrist. His skin was hot against hers, and she sucked air, surprised by his unwanted touch.

"Farrah, wait. There's something you should know."

She rolled her eyes, because was this the moment when Brad would confess the truth?

"What is it?"

"I...I might be sick, Far." He looked up at her with pain slashing across his face. "I might have cancer."

## Chapter Eight

FARRAH

Possible prostate cancer, he'd told her. He'd find out soon.
Farrah had stayed a few more minutes and let him explain, but before they'd parted ways, he'd suggested that she'd left him because she was running from something more than she was afraid that he was cheating.

That was preposterous. Of course she had issues trusting him.

But was it the whole truth? Was Farrah simply bored in her life and wanted to feel a little excitement? She'd been a good wife for years. She'd even accepted that Brad had been unfaithful without announcing his affair publicly. But had that anger swelled deep inside of her until it finally exploded under the pressure?

If she was running, it was because of that, and not for anything else.

Farrah had gotten married young and had done everything that she was supposed to—have kids, raise them, create a beautiful home, cook lavish meals, love her family and her husband.

The thanks that she'd gotten for it was him cheating. She'd pushed that sorrow so far down into the depths of her soul that she'd nearly forgotten that it existed. And it wasn't until she spotted the text on Brad's phone that it all came rushing back with gale-force winds.

She hadn't even meant to see it. Farrah hadn't been spying. His phone had pinged on Thursday morning of Thanksgiving, and she figured it was one of the kids wishing him a happy Thanksgiving since neither of them were going to make it home for the holiday. So she checked it, and that was when she spotted the text.

Now why would anyone text on Thanksgiving morning that they couldn't wait to get back together with him? That was what she thought, and it made sense. No business associate would do such a thing.

Of course not.

So she left. She packed a small suitcase while he was still in the bathroom and walked out, leaving the turkey in the oven.

Brad had called her within thirty minutes, but she was well on her way to Birmingham by that point. She'd explained that she saw the text, told him to have a great Thanksgiving dinner, and hung up.

She didn't answer his calls for three days.

At that point she thought that maybe, just maybe she'd feel differently, that she'd be ready to speak with him.

But she wasn't. Not at all. In fact, she felt free, unencumbered by the life that she had lived. Farrah felt free to do whatever she wanted. Her kids had called her, of course, and she'd told them that she needed space from their father.

And she told them that she and their father were going through a rough patch and she needed to figure some things out.

That was all. She wouldn't hurt them with the knowledge of his previous infidelity. She couldn't do that to them or to him.

And part of her wanted to *want* to return to Buckhead. She really did. But when Farrah tried to tap into those feelings, she found that they didn't exist.

She wanted to be free.

But then Brad showed up and told her he might have cancer. He might die. How did she feel about that?

Sad, of course. But she didn't want to return to their old life and be his nursemaid because there wasn't anyone else for him to rely on.

She'd been his maid and a nanny all her life. She wanted to be his partner.

When Farrah thought about it, that was at the crux of her problem. She didn't feel like Ginny had with Jack—completely unappreciated. Brad appreciated her, she knew that. But Brad didn't fight for her. He took her for granted, not seeming to care if she was around or not.

Farrah needed more than that.

She wanted to feel needed, and not because he was dying of cancer. She wanted to feel like she was Brad's air, his water, his nourishment—everything that kept him alive.

But right now, all she felt was that he'd chased her because he was worried about himself, not because he couldn't live without her.

And that was what hurt the worst.

But for some reason, at lunch, she wasn't able to express that. She felt trapped with Brad's revelation about his prostate. How could she explain to him that she felt underappreciated when he might be dying? It didn't seem justified to be selfish in that moment.

Yes, she'd been selfish in leaving him and running to Sugar Cove. But taking his possible cancer diagnosis and turning that into a life lesson for him was foolish.

So all she'd said when they left was that she was sorry and that she would be there, in Sugar Cove, if he needed her.

That was all.

Yes, his expression had fallen. He'd been clearly upset by her statement, but she'd said what she meant. She would be here for him, and if he needed anything, to let her know.

Farrah was thinking about all these things when she spotted *that woman*, Savannah, stepping out of a hair salon.

She was still in the area? Why on earth was that woman here and not back in Buckhead, where she belonged, living out Ginny's life?

Farrah suspected that more was going on with Savannah than she'd told Ginny, and where there was a mystery, there was Farrah wanting to get to the bottom of it.

But how was she supposed to get information without seeming sneaky? Well, there might not be a way to do that. Farrah would probably have to dive right in.

Lucky for her, Savannah was heading in her direction. They'd pass each other on the street. This was the perfect opportunity to get her mind off Brad and onto something else—which was also why she'd been going crazy decorating for Christmas. It kept her from thinking too much about her husband.

She pretended to not be paying attention to where she was walking and accidentally-on-purpose walked right into Savannah.

"Oh, I'm so sorry," she squealed.

Savannah took a step back, surprise filling her eyes. "Oh! That's okay."

Her gaze latched on to Farrah, and recognition instantly flared in her eyes. "You're..."

"Farrah. I lived in Buckhead, not far from you. You took over the Rigby home."

"Yes." Then she peered deeper into Farrah's eyes. "You're Ginny's friend."

"That's right. I am. And you came here to get Ginny to take her old house back."

She swallowed, and a lump bobbed in her throat. "That's right. I want to give it back."

Farrah tipped her head to the left and right, studying Savannah. There was something uneasy about the woman, something *off*. "You told my friend you want to give it back to her because you can't make any friends. But that's not the truth, is it?"

"Of course it is," Savannah said with a scoff. "Why would I lie?"

"Because you weren't too worried about making friends when you slept with Jack and had his baby, now were you?"

Savannah's jaw dropped. "How dare you?"

"How dare I, what? Say the truth? Southerners might be known for their politeness, but sometimes a good Christian woman has to look a liar in the face and call her a liar. Now, maybe you should tell me exactly why you want to give up that house—that's if you want a shot of actually being able to get it off your hands."

Tears pricked her eyes. "Is there someplace we can go to talk?"

A slow smile crept over Farrah's face. "Why, of course there is. Follow me."

\* \* \*

Farrah told Savannah about a boardwalk overlooking the bay. Savannah followed Farrah in her car, of course. She wasn't interested in getting in the same vehicle with *that woman,* and she also couldn't help but notice that the car Savannah drove was expensive—foreign. Not your usual foreign car, but definitely high-end.

Jack would've rather died than watch Ginny drive anything that expensive, and she'd had a Germany-manufactured Mercedes.

And for that matter, now that Farrah thought about it, Savannah's hair looked very expensive, too. These weren't just a few highlights slapped into her tresses. No, these were well placed by someone who knew what they were doing.

She had a suspicion that she understood exactly why Savannah wanted to sell Ginny that house, but she needed the woman to confirm it.

After Farrah parked and met Savannah on the small boardwalk, she made sure to get a good look at her jewelry and clothing. The clothes were well made and fit her like a glove. There was probably some tailoring that had ensued to make sure that they fit appropriately. As her mother used to say, there was nothing a good tailor couldn't fix—at least when it came to clothes.

And the watch that Savannah wore was gold, inset with diamonds. If she wasn't mistaken, she knew that yes, the piece was real. More parts of the puzzle were beginning to snap together.

They walked for a few minutes before Farrah finally got tired of Savannah's silence, so she started first. "Don't you think that you've hurt my friend enough?"

Savannah closed her eyes momentarily and exhaled. "I never meant to hurt anybody."

At that, Farrah threw her head back and laughed. "You should've thought about that before you slept with a married man."

Savannah stopped and whipped toward Farrah. "Look, I know that I've made a lot of wrong choices, but I wouldn't trade my child for any of them. You can judge me all that you want to—go ahead, but you met me here, remember? You wanted to know why I'd like to sell the house to Ginny. Do you still want to know that, or are you more interested in condemning me more than I've already condemned myself?"

Her words struck Farrah as hard as any slap. "I suppose you're right. You should be given a chance to say your piece. Go ahead. I'm listening."

"Thank you." Savannah pinched the bridge of her nose before continuing. "I'm a hair stylist. That's how Jack and I met. I would cut his hair. We became close, but it took months before that ever happened. And to be honest, I tried not to like him. I tried not to be attracted to him, but in the end I just gave in to my attraction. Yes, I should be ashamed of myself. But I'm not. Not anymore. I'm ashamed of the pain that I've caused Ginny and her family. Don't think I'm not. But if I'm to keep moving forward in life, I can't be ashamed. I have to look to the future." She exhaled heavily. "But anyway, I was just a hair dresser from a trailer park when I met Jack. We never had money when I was growing up, so when I got pregnant, of course he told me to quit my job and start getting ready for the baby—that he'd take care of everything. So I did, and he did."

There was a long pause, and Farrah spoke for her. "But then Jack passed away."

Savannah's throat bobbed. She stopped walking and put her hands on the guardrail, glancing out into the bay. Tall grass waved in the sea breeze, and the briny air trickled up Farrah's nose. She could understand why Ginny had moved here, why she might not ever leave. Everything was slower at the beach—the lifestyle, the worries. They didn't take over your life in the same stressful way that they did when you lived in the congestion of the city.

"But then Jack passed away," Savannah repeated, "and everything changed." She turned around to face the walking trail, leaning her back against the railing. "I was given this big house and lots of money. With the grieving and all the new responsibilities, as well as meeting people in the neighborhood—people who thought I was a harlot, for lack of a better word—it's all been a bit much."

"So you started spending," Farrah filled in.

Savannah's gaze darted to hers, and she slowly nodded. Tears brimmed in her eyes, and she knuckled them away before they could leak onto her cheeks.

"I started spending. At first it was mainly due to grief. There was so much money in the accounts. I could never spend it all in one lifetime. I thought a new car would make me feel better, so I got one. Then I realized that all the other ladies in Buckhead dressed differently from me, so I tracked down where they shopped. At first my eyes almost popped out of my head when I saw how expensive the clothes were." She threw her head back and laughed. "But I thought, if this is where they shop, and I want to fit in, then I'd better shop here, too. I thought that maybe I'd make friends if I could look like them. So I bought lots of clothes."

"There went ten grand," Farrah mused.

She knew how expensive those private boutiques were. Ginny had never been a patron to any of them when she was married to Jack unless she needed an outfit for a special occasion.

Blouses that cost five hundred dollars, pants that cost the same. And dresses? Those usually started at a grand a pop.

"And the clothes were so beautiful," Savannah agreed. "Before I knew it, I was going in once a week to see what was new. They knew my taste and started pulling things for me to look at. They'd offer me champagne when I arrived."

"And what about your son? Where was he when you were doing all this spending?"

"Either at school, or sports, or with my mom. She moved in."

Farrah quirked a brow at that. "And what did she think of all the shopping?"

Savannah's mouth tipped up into a bitter smile. "She thought that I should stop, that I was wasting money. But I told her that I was grieving and that soon it would end. I just had to look the part of Jack's widowed mistress."

That was one way to put it, Farrah thought.

"And little by little, bit by bit, all those shopping trips, all the time when I'd buy things that I thought didn't matter—it all started adding up until I realized that the money was gone."

Gone. There was no telling how much Jack had left her. According to Ginny, she'd only just been willed enough to buy the lighthouse. Savannah had gotten the rest of it—plus the house.

The woman dropped her head into her hands. "I know," she said, the sound muffled, before she tipped her head back to look at Farrah. "I know that I was silly and foolish. I wasted what could've lasted me a lifetime, and what do I have to show for it? A bunch of Instagram followers and a house full of stuff."

Ah, Farrah understood a little bit better now. She knew from her daughter that there were influencers who built a life on making their followers jealous because of their luxurious lifestyle. Savannah, in dealing with her grief, had probably done something similar—posted lavish pictures of her eating at restaurants, going to the spa, dressed up in beautiful clothing—when she should have been taking care of her son and going to his sports matches.

She'd built a life on sand instead of building it on rocks, and now it was all washing out from under her.

"So you see," she told Farrah. "I've got to sell the house, and I thought that selling it to Ginny would be the easiest and fastest way to get the money I need. I'll sell it and go back to South Carolina, where I'm from, and I'll save every penny that I make from the house to make sure it all goes to my son."

She sounded earnest, and looked the part, too. For the boy's sake Farrah hoped so, but it never hurt a person to hear a little advice. "You could put the money in a trust for him. That would be something. Then you wouldn't have access to it, so you wouldn't be tempted to spend it on yourself. It would all go to your child." She sighed. "You may not want to hear this, but it's what Jack would've wanted. He would've wanted his son taken care of above all else."

Savannah's gaze dropped to the ground. "You're right. I've really screwed everything up so far." She pressed the heels of her hands into her eyes and released a shaky sob. "I just hope that I can make it all right."

Well, that was impossible. She'd caused too much hurt to ever be able to completely heal the wounds she'd cut into Ginny and her girls, but time was a helpful thing.

Against her better judgment, Farrah squeezed Savannah's shoulder, and wasn't expecting it when the woman threw herself into Farrah's arms for a hug.

"Oh, okay." Farrah sighed before slowly circling her arms around the woman and squeezing.

Ginny would kill her if she knew they were hugging. But then again, maybe she wouldn't. Savannah was as broken as Ginny was when her life had been flipped upside down. Perhaps she would recognize that what Savannah needed was a friend, because she obviously didn't have one back in Georgia.

"It's going to be okay," she told Savannah, who after a time, quieted her sniffles and pulled away, swiping streaking tears from her cheeks.

She forced a smile. "I know. I just never expected anything to be this hard. When I got together with Jack, things were complicated; *that* I was prepared for. But I never expected the rest of it. Never expected that I'd burn through so much money and be left with nothing more than a huge, empty house."

"But it's worth quite a bit if sold," Farrah reminded her. "That money would be enough for you to live comfortably on if you put yourself on a budget. It would also be enough for a wonderful trust for your son's education and his life, if you chose to use the money for that."

Savannah swallowed hard. "Yeah, you're right."

Would she take Farrah's advice? She certainly hoped so. But neither of them said a word as they quietly headed back to their respective cars.

In fact, it wasn't until Farrah was standing in front of her door that Savannah blurted out, "So do you think Ginny will buy my house? You'll tell her why I need her help, won't you? You'll make her see that it's the best thing for her. I mean, I could sell it on the open market, of course, but I wanted to give her the first shot at it. That way, maybe I can sleep a little better at night, knowing that I've tried to do at least *one* right thing. The past can't be taken back. There's no making up for what happened with Jack. But if I could give Ginny her old life back, that would be something. It would mean something to me."

Farrah slowly nodded as she opened her car door. "Yes, it would mean something," she agreed. "It would definitely mean something."

But would it be enough of a peace offering that Ginny would take it? Only Ginny held the answer to that question.

# Chapter Nine

It was impossible for Ginny not to be worried, because in the past week the restaurant had gone from packed to the gills to a desolate wasteland.

It made her seriously consider Savannah's offer. How easy would it be to close the shop, sell the place and move home? Return to the life and the people that she knew. It would be like slipping into a pair of old shoes. They were already broken in, and she knew they would be comfortable. This would be the same.

But as tempting as it was, Ginny had a life here, and she wasn't going to simply jump ship. However, if business didn't pick up, and soon, she would have to sell. There was no way around that.

She kept her fears hidden from her daughters, though. There was no point in having them worry. But even though she tried to hide things from them, they were smart and didn't miss much.

"Maybe we should open up a food truck," Reece said in passing one morning. "That way we can travel wherever we need to in order to make money."

Ginny grimaced. "Do things look that bad?"

"They look kinda bad." Her daughter hefted a tray of glass dishes filled with banana pudding into the refrigerator. "I just don't get it. What's going on?"

She gritted her teeth. "I'd like to know, too."

And that was all they said about it until it was time to open, and the first customer of the day was Aiden, who beamed when he saw Ginny.

Well, beaming was the first thing he did. The second was to scan the dining room and frown. "Where is everybody?"

She rested her hip on the counter. "It's been like this for nearly two weeks."

"Huh. That doesn't seem right."

"You and I agree on that."

"But the Christmas decorations look good."

"At least one thing does," she grumbled.

Aiden's expression fell. "Things'll pick up. It's probably just folks saving up for Christmas."

"That didn't stop them from eating in Port St. Joe the other day," Farrah said as she swooped into the dining room.

Her best friend smiled at them, but ever since she'd come back from her day excursion, Farrah had been distant. Ginny had tried to get whatever secret she was keeping out of her, but her best friend had kept quiet. She had also stopped decorating for Christmas, which relieved Ginny. However, that hadn't stopped Farrah from rearranging everything in the one small bathroom they all shared—giving everyone their own spots for toothbrushes and makeup. Ginny had been relegated to a small spot to the left of the sink.

Even though Farrah was going through personal issues, they'd need to have a talk sooner or later about their living arrangements.

"Is there any lunch?" Aiden asked.

Ginny smiled. "There's as much as you'd like."

She fixed him a plate and talked with him while he ate. "So there are a lot of things that happen this time of year around here," he told her.

"Oh? What sort of things?"

"Well, the Chamber of Commerce sponsors a dance."

"Yeah?" She folded her arms and used all her willpower not to grin. She didn't succeed. "A dance, huh? What sort of dance? Are we talking a sock hop? Ballroom? Maybe a rave?"

He laughed. "It's definitely not a rave or a sock hop. It's a few days before Christmas, and usually the whole town comes out."

"The whole town, huh? That sounds like quite a big deal."

"It's not that big a deal."

"Well, I don't know, if the whole town is there, it might be."

He rolled his eyes at her teasing. "Okay, it's kind of a big deal, and I was wondering if you'd like to go with me."

"Hm." She pretended to think about it. "And how should I go with you? As your friend? As your special guest? Maybe as the lunch lady?"

He threw his head back and laughed. "Definitely not as the lunch lady. I'd like for you to come with me as my date."

She glanced over her shoulder to make sure that her daughters didn't hear. They were busy with the two other customers who had entered while she'd been distracted by Aiden's presence.

It was easy to be distracted by him with his rugged good looks and charm. But not so distracted that she didn't remember that he'd asked her a question.

"Since you've asked so nicely, yes, I would love to go as your date."

"Great."

He gave her the details and told her what time he'd pick her up. The ball was only a little over a week away, which meant that there was little time to find a dress and make alterations to it if she needed to. But then again, she might have something in her closet, from her old life, that would do.

"And how fancy am I supposed to dress?"

"As fancy as you'd like," he told her.

"Don't tell me that." She laughed. "I might show up wearing puffy sleeves and a ball gown."

He shrugged. "If you did, I'm sure you'd look beautiful in it." Her heart warmed at his words. He rose from the chair and smiled kindly. "Whatever you wear, I'm sure it'll be perfect."

"I'll see if I can find something."

"Like I said, don't worry about it too much. Whatever you put on will be beautiful."

After he paid, they said goodbye and Aiden left. The lunch crowd was still small, but from the windows she spotted folks at Vera's gas station. Folks weren't just getting gas. They were inside picking over Vera's lunch selection, which was a staple in Sugar Cove. Vera served the best hamburgers in town, and Ginny knew today was no exception.

Vera also knew everyone. If there was gossip to be heard, Vera would be the person to grab it from.

She told Farrah that she'd be back, and then Ginny pulled a light sweater on and headed across the street.

She had been right about the gas station. Inside, the store was buzzing with activity. Shelby, Vera's granddaughter and Reece's best friend, sat at the front register and waved to Ginny when she entered.

"Hey, Ginny! How're things at the café?"

"Oh, just fine," she replied as any good Southern woman would.

In the South it wasn't uncommon to simply be polite in answering and tell a person that everything was okay even if it wasn't. Everyone knew that when a person asked how you were doing, that didn't mean that they actually wanted to know. They simply wanted to hear that everything was well and let that be the end of it.

She made her way to the food counter and waited in line while construction workers grabbed cheeseburgers and corn dogs that were wrapped and ready to take. Vera stood with her back to the counter, working the grill.

Ginny approached the counter and greeted her. "Hey, Vera. How're you?"

The older woman slowly turned around. Her mouth split into a wide smile when she spotted Ginny. Vera looked like a quintessential grandmother with her gray hair and round body. She wasn't too round. The older woman seemed to get around okay, and she was just soft enough that Ginny was certain she gave good hugs.

"I'm great, Ginny. How're things going with you?"

She cringed. "Well, actually. That's what I came to talk to you about. I'm wondering if you could spare a few minutes?"

"For you—anytime. Give me some time to finish these patties and I'll come out."

Five minutes later Vera walked out from behind the counter with a bottle of water in one hand. She motioned toward one of the two booths that were inside the gas station, and Ginny followed.

Vera sat and exhaled. "These folks are working me to death in here."

Her words were hard, but her tone was soft. Ginny knew that everyone in life needed a job. People needed something to keep them busy, and she suspected that Vera wouldn't have things any other way.

"What can I do for you?" the older woman said.

Now that Ginny was here, she wasn't sure how to ask her question, but she decided that simply spitting it out would be the best way to go about it.

"For the past week, things at the café have taken a nosedive. It's the strangest thing. One week we were so busy that I could barely think, and now—well, if this keeps up, we won't be able to keep the lights on three months from now. I just can't figure out what it is."

"Hm." Vera ran a hand over her mouth. "I'm sorry to hear all of this."

"I'm sorry to be telling you any of it. But..." She tried to find the words. "It's just so strange. Last weekend I was in Port St. Joe doing some shopping. I introduced myself to a business owner when my friend was paying for some ornaments. The owner moved away, and when I looked over at her a few seconds later, she was whispering to someone and staring at me."

Vera's eyes narrowed. "Is that so?"

"Yes." She sighed. "I can't help to think that the two are connected, but it also seems so ridiculous, so outlandish. Is it possible that there's a connection? Or am I just losing my mind?"

"No, I don't think you're losing your mind." She tapped her fingers on the table. "I never thought things would wind up like this," she muttered, more to herself than to Ginny.

"Never thought *what* would end up like this?"

The shop owner shook her head and sighed. "Ginny, there are some things you need to know about this town, or about Aiden in particular."

Her back snapped to attention. "Aiden? What's he got to do with anything?"

Vera patted the air. "Now, calm down. I don't mean him directly, but more indirectly."

An edge that she wasn't able to soften filled her words. "Can you please explain?"

"Now don't shoot the messenger, but what I'm going to tell you will help things make sense. You probably know that he was married to a woman named Ellen."

"Yes, I know about her and why they divorced."

"You can't keep much a secret in a small town. We all know that Ellen likes to spend money. I don't suppose anything has changed on that front. She drives a pretty fancy car."

"That she does."

"But anyway, it's well-known around here, to us locals, that she's never gotten over him. From what I hear, every once in a while she calls him or writes him an email or letter, something like that, trying to get back together."

A pit opened in her stomach. "I didn't know that."

"I'm not saying this because you've got something to worry about. I don't think that at all. I'm just telling you what kind of woman she is. No matter how many times Aiden tells her that he's not interested, she doesn't listen."

"Okay," she said slowly, "but what's this have to do with me?"

"Well"—Vera sighed heavily—"you're the first woman that he's really dated since the divorce. I'm sure there have been other casual relationships, but no one like you—no one who he's been seen around town with."

That sparked a flare of pride in her chest. "I'm still not following."

"You're about to be, because from what I've heard, Ellen's not too happy that the two of y'all are so lovey-dovey, and I don't think it's a coincidence that a rumor has started."

A tingle of worry started at Ginny's head and crawled down her back one vertebra at a time. "What sort of rumor?"

Vera gave her a sharp look. "The kind where people think your café has given half the town food poisoning."

## Chapter Ten

To say that Ginny was angry was an understatement like no other. She was more than angry. She was furious.

As she walked out of Vera's gas station, fury roiled through her blood like lava, making her hands burn.

How could Ellen do something so horrible? How could she start a vicious rumor that Ginny's food had poisoned people? It wasn't only a terrible thing to do. This was playing with Ginny's livelihood. She needed every cent that people paid for her food in order to keep her business going, pay her daughters, eat, warm her lighthouse. To put it bluntly, she needed the money to live. Period.

And Ellen was doing her best to snatch that out from under Ginny's feet.

There was no way that she would allow that to happen.

She didn't bother returning to the café for lunch. Instead she got into her car and headed for Port St. Joe.

The drive gave her a chance to think. She imagined walking into the real estate agency and seeing Ellen.

But before words could come to her, that blinding rage took over again.

Why was it so hard to live a good life? Why couldn't things just be easy? Why did troublesome people have to follow wherever Ginny went?

Jack had dictated her life, and for the first time Ginny was in control

A LIGHTHOUSE CHRISTMAS

—or so she thought. But now someone was trying to ruin her and for no reason other than the fact that she was dating the woman's ex-husband.

*Ex.*

They weren't even married anymore.

At that thought her phone buzzed. She looked down and saw Aiden's name flashing on the screen.

She reached for her phone and stopped, her fingers curled to take it into her hand. Was telling him about Ellen the best thing? He would want to come to her rescue. He'd want to talk to his ex himself.

No.

This was something that Ginny had to do—stand on her own two legs and confront the person harming her. She didn't need to hide behind anyone.

She reached the real estate building and parked, taking a minute to inhale and exhale. One look in the mirror told her that there was no hiding how upset she was. Her neck and cheeks were flushed, clearly a sign of emotional stress.

Well, she *was* stressed. There was no point in denying it.

Before she got out of the car, she made sure that she looked as nice as possible. Her hair was up, as it always was when she was working. Her makeup was flawless, and she added a new coat of lipstick, because her mother had always taught her that even if you didn't have any other makeup on, a coat of lipstick did wonders for your face.

Ginny knew she was right.

After one last look in the rearview mirror, she stepped out of the car, squared her shoulders and headed inside.

The office was quiet when she walked in. A few agents sat at cubicles, talking on their phones. It occurred to Ginny that nowadays agents probably didn't need to be in an office. Their home computers had the software needed to search for homes.

When a young man got off the phone, he spotted Ginny and gave her a wide, pearly smile. "How can I help you?"

"I'm looking for Ellen."

His brow wrinkled as if he knew that he'd just lost a sale. "Oh, Ellen? She's not here."

He nodded to the woman across the cubicle. "Do you know if Ellen's coming in today?"

The woman clicked her tongue. "She's got an agent open house." She checked her watch. "She's probably just finishing up."

"What's the address?" Ginny asked.

The woman gave it to her, and Ginny thanked her. Then she quickly left the agency before anyone could ask her why she needed to speak with Ellen.

* * *

Ellen was, indeed, finishing up the agent showing when Ginny arrived. A few people dressed smartly were trickling from the house, brochures in hand.

It was a grand beach mansion just down from the agency, prime location for a family who wanted a second home that they could also rent out when they weren't occupying it.

As Ginny stepped up the walkway, Ellen was coming out of the door and had turned to lock it. She hadn't spotted Ginny yet. So she took a moment to study the agent—her lithe frame, her well-tailored clothing. Just seeing the woman made a shock wave rock through Ginny's body.

Her hands went clammy, and her mind became blank as a sheet of paper.

What was she going to say? How would she prove the improvable?

Before any of those answers struck her, Ellen turned around, spotted her and shook her head. "Sorry, you just missed the tour, but I do have more brochures."

She reached into her black leather satchel to grab one, but Ginny's cold voice stopped her. "I'm not here for a tour."

Ellen's body went rigid as she slowly peeled her gaze from the satchel and lifted it until it landed on Ginny. Her jaw tightened.

"Oh, Ginny, owner of the Lighthouse Café. How're you?" she said in a voice as friendly as a snake's.

Ginny halted when she was about four feet from Ellen. The woman was immaculately dressed in a white suit jacket with beaded trim that buttoned just below the shoulder and a matching skirt that screamed elegance.

Ellen didn't look like a terrible person who started lies, but Ginny wasn't about to let first, or even third impressions stop what she had to say.

"The café," Ginny said in reply to her question, "isn't doing that great, actually."

Ellen's brow wrinkled in what Ginny knew to be mock worry. "It isn't? I'm sorry to hear that. Well, if you need to buy a smaller property, let me know."

Ellen started to walk around her, but Ginny blocked her path. "You know why it's not doing well."

"I'm afraid that I don't know what you're talking about. Now, if you'll excuse me."

"No, I won't excuse you."

Ellen balked. "I'm sorry?"

Ginny steeled herself, for not in her entire life had she ever said to someone what she was about to say. Never in her life had she confronted someone like this. But even an old dog could learn new tricks, and standing up for herself was about to be one of them.

"You have told half this town that my restaurant caused food poisoning."

She scoffed. "What would ever make you say—"

"Don't deny it," Ginny gritted out. "I know for a fact what you've done. You're trying to ruin my business because of Aiden."

Out of Ellen's mouth shot the fakest laugh that Ginny had ever heard. "That's ridiculous."

"Is it?" She folded her arms and scowled. "At the Christmas fair you said something about poisoning, and the next thing I know, my customers are dropping like flies. It turns out that all I had to do was ask a few people the right questions and they knew who the culprit was—you. Listen, Ellen, I don't have a problem with you. Or at least I didn't until now. But I can tell you that if Aiden had wanted to get back together with you, he would've done it a long time ago."

The agent's face twisted in anger. "Keep him out of this. You don't know a thing about our relationship."

"You're right. I don't. All I know is what he's told me—that you spent his money faster than he could earn it. But look at how successful you are. You are truly one of the top real estate agents in this area. But yet you're a nasty person on the inside. Most of us are just trying to live our lives."

She took a breath. "I spent half of my life married to a man who dictated how much money I could have and how it was spent. For the first time that control is mine and mine alone. Now you come along and try to snatch my freedom away. Well, I'm not going to stand for it. It's not right, and you know that. Even though you want to be mean and nasty, you know that it isn't the right thing to do. So take it back, Ellen. Tell this town and Sugar Cove that you lied, that you made up the story about my café."

Ellen stared at her for a long moment as if she was deliberating on whether or not to admit what she had done. When she finally spoke, she simply said, "If your restaurant gave people food poisoning, that's on you. Not me. I didn't have anything to do with it."

So she wanted to play that way, did she? "I'm not going to back down without a fight. I'm not going to slink off into the sunset so that Aiden's free and you can swoop in and attempt to take him. Even if you did, he wouldn't go with you. You won't get him. Doing this to me won't endear you to him, I can promise you that."

Ellen scoffed. "Are you threatening me?"

Ginny took a step closer. "You mean threatening to take your livelihood away, destroy your life and ruin you? No, I'm not sinking to your level. I have no intention of doing that. But what I do intend is not to let you win."

"Good luck," Ellen muttered as she stepped around Ginny and headed for her car.

This didn't feel like a victory, but it didn't feel like a defeat, either. Ginny turned and headed to her own car, watching as Ellen glanced over her shoulder and shot Ginny a hard look.

Ginny almost laughed. She could shoot her as many dirty looks as she wanted, but that wasn't going to change anything. Ginny didn't have a plan, but that didn't mean she wasn't going to come up with one. She could do that with the help of her family, because three heads, or even four, counting Farrah, were better than one.

# Chapter Eleven

"She did *what?*" Reece said later that night at the dinner table.

They were trying to keep costs down, so Reece had created a simple dinner of sausage and chicken gumbo, filled with plenty of okra. The broth was a dark ribbon the color of chocolate, and Reece had spent the better part of the afternoon making the roux, which she stirred and stirred for over an hour as she patiently waited for it to turn dark brown. It was only then that she added broth and the other ingredients, letting it simmer for another hour until it was ready.

Chandler had arrived with a loaf of crusty French bread, and Ginny had opened a bottle of red wine. Farrah had dug out expensive chocolates from her suitcase—her *emergency food supply*, as she had jokingly called it.

But in Ginny's opinion, this was an emergency. It was an emergency, indeed.

In answer to Reece's question, Ginny restated, "Ellen is telling the town that our café is giving people food poisoning."

Farrah slumped back in her chair. "You mean that's why those two women were staring at you when we went shopping?"

"That's why."

She felt three pairs of eyes on her, so Ginny took a sip of the gumbo. The roux was perfect, a rich, savory broth that was made extra special with the okra. If you didn't have okra in a gumbo, then it wasn't gumbo in her opinion.

Reece dragged the bread through the broth. "That's just plain evil. Who does that?"

"Jealous people," Chandler murmured, sipping her wine.

"Exactly," Farrah chimed. "But what do we do about it?"

"Y'all tell me." Ginny raked her fingers through her hair. "Because it's Christmas and fighting fire with fire isn't exactly the theme of this season."

Farrah's gaze swept to the decorations that surrounded them. "No, it sure isn't. But at the same time we can't let this go. It'll ruin you. You have to do something to stop the rumors."

"I know."

"Maybe you should talk to Aiden," Chandler offered.

"And tell him what? That his ex-wife is trying to destroy me? That I need him to take care of me?"

"No, but it wouldn't hurt if he knew what she'd done," Farrah said, sipping a spoonful of gumbo. "You don't know if this'll be her last attack. If you and Aiden keep dating, what else will she do?"

"Hm. You've got a point."

"She does," Chandler said softly. "But if you don't decide to talk to Aiden, I can understand that, which means you'll be dealing with this on your own, and in that case, you need a way to get the business back on track."

Reece scoffed. "Putting up a sign that says, 'no food poisoning here' isn't the best idea."

"No, but maybe we do things the old-fashioned way."

"What's that?" Reece asked, her nose crinkling.

"Make a flyer and go door to door, get folks thinking about our café at lunch," Chandler told her. "Reece and I can hand them out before lunchtime Monday morning. You'll have a packed house for the first service, I can promise you that."

Ginny considered the plan. As much as she'd love to get back at Ellen by putting an ad in the paper proclaiming that Ellen was a liar, it wasn't a nice thing to do. It wasn't ladylike, and it could, in fact, just add gasoline to the fire. Yes, handing out flyers and pulling in business the old-fashioned way might be a plan worth exploring.

But on the other hand, "What's to stop her from doing something like this again?"

"That's where you need to bring Aiden in," her best friend counseled. "He'll have to talk to Ellen and tell her to lay off. There's just no other way around it."

Ginny groaned. "I really didn't want to tell him about this."

"We know that fighting your own battles is important to you, but you also have to know when to ask for help, and now is the time. This woman is intent on destroying your business, Ginny. Planting a rumor that your café is poisoning people isn't a small deal. It's a very, very big deal. You can't just walk away from that. You've got to tell Aiden. He deserves to know."

"And speaking of men deserving to know this," Reece said, flashing a big smile, "what about Uncle Brad?"

"Aren't you too young to be asking me questions like that?"

"No, I'm not. Chandler and I are at the grown-up's table now. We need to know things."

Farrah and Ginny laughed. But just as quickly as their laughter ended, Ginny turned to her friend. "She's got a point. Have you talked to him?"

Farrah sighed. "I ran into him the other day."

"And?"

"And we had lunch, and he told me that he may have prostate cancer."

The three women's jaws dropped. "Farrah, no!" Ginny cried. "Is he okay?"

"He's okay, just bracing himself for bad news, like any of us would be. He's worried and scared."

"So this means you'll be moving back in with him, right?"

"It doesn't. I'm not running back."

It felt like Ginny had been punched in the gut. "What? But this is serious."

Farrah closed her eyes and exhaled. "There are things that I've never told you about our relationship."

"Okay," her friend slowly said. "Like what?"

"Like, about five years ago, he had an affair."

"Not Uncle Brad!"

"Reece," Chandler chided. "Let her talk."

"Honey, why didn't you tell me?" Ginny asked her.

To say that Ginny was hurt was only touching the tip of the iceberg. She was deeply wounded that her friend had never mentioned a word of this to her. Why hadn't Farrah felt comfortable confiding in her?

"The reason I never said anything is because, well, I don't know. I didn't want my marriage to become some stereotype. The husband gets bored, so he cheats."

"But you didn't even tell me after what Jack did to me," Ginny said in a voice more accusing than she meant it to be.

"It wasn't right for me to take your situation and turn it onto myself. This was your time of mourning, and I needed to be there for you. But anyway, what's done is done. Brad ended the relationship and we moved on—until I found that text where the person said that they couldn't wait to meet up with him. Now what am I supposed to think? That was just some party planner he was talking to?"

Ginny took the last bite of her gumbo and pushed the bowl away. "Let me ask you this—how did you find out about his previous affair?"

"I found panties," she grumbled.

"And when you confronted him, did Brad admit things right off?"

"He had to. I had evidence."

"He could've still tried to deny it," Ginny pointed out. "He wouldn't be the first man to find some stupid explanation for a pair of panties in his drawer."

"Yeah, he could've tried to gaslight you," Reece added. "Tell you that they're yours and you put them in his drawer by mistake."

Farrah shook her head. "I wouldn't have bought them, and he knew that."

"Just like you wouldn't buy it now that he's cheating on you," Ginny pointed out. "If Brad had wanted to lie to you, he could. But the first time he had an affair, he didn't. I think that says something for his character. As much as you don't want to hear this, I don't think he's lying. I think he's telling the truth. But it's all up to you on whether or not you choose to believe him."

Farrah sat silently for a minute. "He's never been a very good liar. Maybe you're right. Maybe I should give him some benefit of the doubt. However, I can't leave before the decorating committee judges the café. I've got to see the end result of that competition."

"You deserve to," Ginny told her.

"Thank you." The women laughed, and when it quieted, Farrah said, "There's one more thing that you should know."

"We're on an explosive roll," Reece said. "What could possibly be next?"

"Be careful what you wish for," her older sister scolded. "This could be the biggest news of the night."

"It is," Farrah admitted. "So hold on to your seats, because I talked to *that woman*."

Ginny's eyes became big as plates. "You mean Savannah?"

"The one and only."

"Why?" Reece asked.

"Because no matter what she said, I know she isn't selling Ginny the house to be nice. There's a story there."

Chandler nibbled on a piece of bread. "What is it?"

"Brace yourselves—she's already burned through the money that Jack left her."

"What?" the three women shrieked at the same time.

Ginny sank back onto the chair, the shock of what she'd just learned washing over her. "He left her—well, there's no telling how much money Jack left. And she spent it *all*? How?"

"A luxury car, clothes, there's no telling what else. She wanted to offer the house to you first because she figured that would be the quickest way to get it off her hands."

"It may also partly be a peace offering," Chandler said. "That makes sense. Since there's nothing she can do to apologize to you. I mean, words aren't going to change what she did, so the next best thing is to give— correction, *sell*—the house back to you."

Ginny could barely wrap her head around it. Though she didn't know the exact amount, she knew that Jack had left Savannah a small, if not medium-sized fortune. To think that she'd wasted all that money on frivolous things was, well, mind-blowing. Yet at the same time she understood why.

"She did it to keep up with the Joneses, didn't she?"

"You know how those women like to spend," Farrah quipped. "There's a lot of social pressure to spend, spend, spend, and to spend big."

"I was never given the choice to be able to burn that kind of money," Ginny admitted, "and for once I'm glad for it."

Reece dropped her crumpled paper napkin beside her bowl. "I for one am gobsmacked. She spent all her cash and now wants to sell the house. What's to stop her from burning through all of that, too?"

Farrah tsked. "I suggested she put the money in a trust for her son."

"Our brother," Chandler mused.

"Yeah." Reece's gaze flickered to Ginny. "As much as I'd hate to say this, Savannah's going to be part of our lives, or else we're gonna go through life not knowing our half-brother."

Ginny's heart shattered into a million pieces. Her daughter was right, and she could've spanked herself for not thinking about it before. Her children had a right to know their sibling, and that possibly meant that yes, Savannah and her son would be part of their lives forever. Well, maybe not Ginny's, but certainly Chandler's and Reece's. She couldn't, nor did she want to, keep her children separated from their half-brother. It didn't seem fair.

"What are you going to do, Mama?" Reece asked. "Are you going to buy it?"

There was so much that tempted Ginny to purchase that house. In the past few months she'd learned how to stand on her own two feet. She could move to Atlanta, take out a second mortgage on the home and use the money to rent a small space where she could cook up food similar to what the lighthouse served. The idea was so tantalizing that she could nearly taste it.

After all, that way she wouldn't have to deal with pesky people like Ellen. But then again, there would always be an Ellen in one form or another, a person who was ready to throw a monkey wrench into the gears of her life. She had to be prepared to deal with obstacles like that on her own instead of running from them.

Because when she'd moved to the lighthouse, she'd been running *to* something. She hadn't known it at the time, but now she could look back and see that she had been running to a new life, a new chapter.

And if she returned to Atlanta, would she be running from something in Sugar Cove, or would she be running to the comfort of what she'd known before?

More than that, would that city now be tainted by the sour taste in her mouth she had whenever she thought about Jack? All those happy memories of places they ate at, places they visited, were now shattered because it was all a great big lie.

Was that something that Ginny was willing to risk? She wasn't sure, and of course none of those thoughts even touched on Aiden. She'd been circling around him because, well, it hurt too much to think of leaving this blossoming romance. They were only just getting started, and deep down she felt like he was one of the keys in her new life, a key that unlocked a new chapter, and she was excited to see how it unfolded.

"Mama," Reece said, jolting her from her thoughts. "Earth to Mama, are you in there?"

She chuckled. "Yeah, I'm in here. Just got carried away by my thoughts is all." A sudden wave of fatigue washed over her. "So, is everyone ready to clean up? I'm tired."

Her youngest clicked her tongue. "You didn't answer the question—are you going to buy our old house back? Have you made up your mind?"

A small smile flitted on Ginny's lips. "I've made up my mind."

Chandler shot Reece a worried look. "Well, what are you going to do?"

"First, I'm going to talk to Savannah. Then I'll let the rest of y'all know my plans."

# Chapter Twelve

After dinner was cleaned up, Ginny made two cups of hot tea and met Farrah in the small common room between the two bedrooms. Farrah sat in a chair reading a mystery, and as much as Ginny hated to interrupt, this needed to be done.

"Want to chat?"

Farrah slipped a bookmark between the pages and shut the novel. "Sure. But if this is about Brad—"

"It is."

She rolled her eyes. "Haven't I said everything that I needed to say?"

"Did you? I don't think so." Farrah took the cup of tea that Ginny offered, and Ginny seated herself across from her friend, in an old, overstuffed rocking chair that looked more like a recliner than it did a rocker. She sighed. "So. Why aren't you going to help Brad?"

"I never said that I wasn't going to help him." She sipped her tea and smiled. "Sleepytime. My favorite."

"Mine too." Ginny settled her tea on the table between them and rocked back. "You're right. You never said that you wouldn't help him, but isn't that obvious? You're abandoning him. Your husband tells you that he may have cancer, and what do you do? You're not running home to make sure he's okay; you're leaving him to figure things out on his own. Is that really fair?"

Farrah's eyes pinched in anger. "Is it really fair that he cheated on me?"

"No, of course not. But he admitted it, and that was years ago. If he told you the truth once, don't you think he'd do so again?"

She sighed and settled her mug onto the book in her lap. "I really don't know. I feel like a fool, Ginny. If I just accept what he says about that text, and go back to him only to discover that he really is cheating, then shame on me. I'm the idiot in this situation."

"But if he's not, and he really does need you... Look, all I'm saying is that you worked through a hard time once and didn't bother to tell your best friend about it. I'm not mad, so don't think that I am. It's just that I wonder if there's something else you're afraid of here."

What was it with everyone asking if she was afraid of something? "Why do I have to be scared not to want to go back to him? Why is that? Why can't I just be angry and not want to return?"

Ginny smiled warmly. "Because I know you, remember? It's not like you to back away from a fight. So this means that something else is going on."

Her best friend sighed before dropping her head onto the back of her chair. "What if I go back to Buckhead, spend my life with Brad, only to discover near the end that he has been cheating on me this whole time. What if..." Tears sprouted in her eyes. "What if what happened to you happens to me?"

The words took Ginny by surprise. Her friend's face was flush with nerves, and she understood why.

She could've been angry with Farrah. She could've felt betrayed, but Ginny didn't feel any of those things as she reached across the space and squeezed her friend's arm.

"What Jack did to me is a once-in-a-lifetime event. I don't think lightning will strike twice so close to the both of us ever again. I just don't, and don't feel badly for thinking or saying what you did. You were honest, and to be fair, if you weren't worried that Brad would do something like that, I'd be worried about you." A light laugh flitted from her mouth. "But I trust that he won't, and that he's being honest. Your husband needs you right now, Farrah, and you're doing him, your marriage and yourself a disservice by staying here and not helping him through it."

Farrah's face crumpled for a brief moment before she stilled her features. She exhaled a staggered breath. "You're right. Of course you are. It's just, I don't know. Maybe I was looking for an excuse to leave him before he could hurt me, so when I saw the text, I jumped on it. Sometimes it's easier to run than it is to face your fears."

Ginny smiled sadly. "The truth is, it's always easier to run, but it's never satisfying because you don't know what your life would've turned out like if you hadn't run. So often, regret is chasing you down, holding on to you."

Farrah sighed and tucked a strand of hair behind her ear. "You're right. I don't want to regret not having listened to Brad, and I certainly don't want to have regretted turning my back on him when he needs me most. Besides, our kids would never forgive me if I did."

"No, they won't," she said in agreement. "But what's worse is that I don't think you would ever forgive yourself, either."

"I suppose you're right." She sipped her tea, and when she placed it down, Farrah smiled sadly. "Thank you for giving me a good, swift kick in the rear."

With a laugh she replied, "Sometimes that's what all of us need to wake us up."

"Well, I'm definitely awake now."

"Now you have to talk to Brad and see where you go from here."

"Oh, I'm not leaving Sugar Cove until the Christmas decorating committee arrives and gives you first place in the contest."

"No one can ever say that you aren't optimistic, Farrah."

She winked. "And they shouldn't."

The two women chuckled as they drank their tea and talked about Ginny's plan to turn her business around.

* * *

The next morning Ginny woke up an hour early and opened her computer. She spent half an hour making a flyer highlighting that day's specials and printed out fifty of them.

By the time Chandler arrived to start setting up for the first lunch service, she had the flyers in her hand and gave them to her daughter.

"Go to Port St. Joe and hand these out. Go to every office that you can find, give them to anyone and everyone that you see."

"Will do, Mama."

While Chandler dropped off flyers, Ginny, Reece and Farrah readied for the lunch rush. Or at least Ginny prayed there would be a lunch rush.

When the doors were finally unlocked at eleven, there wasn't anyone banging down the doors waiting for entry. But, little by little, people started to arrive. People that Ginny hadn't seen before—a whole new host of customers! This was what she had wanted and prayed for.

No, it wasn't the onslaught of folks that they usually had on Monday mornings, but it was a start, and it was enough to keep the restaurant in the black—for now.

* * *

"Why've you been so quiet tonight?" Aiden asked later. They'd had dinner out, and Ginny had gone back to his house to watch a movie.

She sat beside him on the couch, and Aiden tapped his lap, indicating that he wanted her feet. She shyly gave them to him, and he pressed into the insoles with his thumbs, firmly but gently massaging the aches away.

She moaned. "A girl could get used to this."

"I want a girl to get used to it."

"I'll gladly take you up on your offer."

"Please do," he replied, hitting a particularly achy spot that made Ginny drop her head onto the back of the couch. "You've been tense all day. Is something going on?"

"No. Yes." She sighed. "I should tell you."

"Yes, you should."

"Oh?" She quirked a brow. "Why's that?"

"Because in case you haven't noticed, you've become important in my life."

It felt like a hand was squeezing her heart so hard that it might pop out of her chest. "You're important in my life, too."

"I'm glad to know that we're each important to one another," he told her, staring into her eyes.

She felt a blush creep up her neck, so she glanced away. "But...you were asking about what's eating at me."

He dropped his gaze to her feet. "Yes, I was. So, what is it?"

"I'm going to tell you, but you're not going to like it."

"You're so sure of that?"

"Oh yeah. I'm sure."

"Hit me, and if I have to beat someone up along the way, I don't have any problem with that." When she didn't laugh, he frowned. "Hey, I was only joking."

"But you're not far off."

Aiden frowned, making a little wrinkle form between his eyes. "Okay, so what's going on?"

She inhaled a deep breath, letting it fill her lungs and hoping that it would offer some courage before she said, "The café hasn't been doing well lately. At first I thought maybe something was going on—the economy, people being too busy with Christmas shopping to eat out, but then it just seemed strange because one day we were selling out and the next I couldn't even give the food away."

She waited for him to ask a question, but Aiden only watched her closely, drinking in the story.

So she continued. "I asked Vera at the gas station what was going on, and she told me—you're not going to like it—but she said that she'd heard Ellen was telling people that the café had given customers food poisoning."

Aiden's face became very still, so still that Ginny wasn't sure that he had heard her. But when she spotted a small muscle in his cheek flexing, she knew the truth. He had indeed heard her. He simply wasn't responding because he was tempering his anger.

"But I'm trying to fix it," she explained. "Chandler went to Port St. Joe today and handed out flyers for the café. Lunch service was stronger, almost back to where it used to be."

"But that's not the point," he said quietly. "The point is that my ex-wife is trying to ruin you, and for no reason other than the fact that you're dating me."

She couldn't argue with that. "I'm not going to let her get the upper hand. She's not going to win. Ellen isn't going to steal my business."

"But she already has. She spread lies about your café, Ginny."

She rubbed his arm to soothe his anger, but she wasn't sure if it made any difference, because Aiden's jaw was working overtime. He was ticked off—more than ticked off. She could tell that he was furious and doing his best to strangle the anger building inside of him.

"I talked to her," she explained.

"You did?" He rubbed a hand down his cheek. "How'd that go?"

"Oh, you know, she denied it, that sort of thing."

"I'm going to talk to her."

"No." Panic clawed up her throat. "Don't do that."

"Why not?"

"Because, then it looks like you're jumping to my rescue, like I can't handle myself."

"Ginny, this isn't some small thing. She's trying to ruin your business. This isn't Ellen telling the other kids on the playground that you have cooties."

"I know." She raked her fingers through her hair. "I know it's not. It's just that I don't want you to get involved. That's what she wants. She's trying to get your attention because she doesn't have it, and getting it by doing something negative is just as important as her winning your attention for doing the right thing. If you ignore her, maybe it'll go away."

"I don't want to ignore her. I want her to go up to every person she told that lie to and tell them that she made it up. Ginny"—he scooted in toward her and cupped her face—"you have come to mean a lot to me, and the thought that anyone would hurt you because we're together makes me want to rip the world apart."

Her heart fluttered in her chest like a caged bird. "It does?"

"It does," he said, smiling, the corners of his eyes crinkling. "*You* make me want to burn down the world to get to you. You've filled my life in a way that no one has before, so as silly as it may seem, I want to protect you. I want that responsibility even if you're not interested in giving it to me. Even if, for some reason, you feel the need to protect yourself."

Emotions swirled in her chest. "You can...you can protect me," she squeaked out.

He smiled. "I know that you don't want me to step into this thing with Ellen, but if you change your mind, you know where to find me."

"Massaging my feet?" she joked.

He threw his head back and roared with laughter. When he finished, he brought his lips to hers and murmured into them, "You'll find me right here, with you."

## Chapter Thirteen

### FARRAH

The days that led up to the Christmas decoration judging were busier than Farrah imagined they would be. Business had finally started picking back up, which was a relief. The last thing that Farrah wanted was for her friend's dream to burst into flames and burn up into a chunk of withered wood.

Luckily that was not to be.

The restaurant had been busy that day, and Farrah, along with Reece and Chandler, were finishing wiping the tables while Ginny was in the back, cooling down the food and preparing to put it in the fridge.

She saw three cars pull into the parking lot, and she just knew who was going to step out of them. "Girls, the decorating committee is here! They've arrived. How does everything look?"

Reece's gaze swept over the decor. "Amazing. You're going to win first place for sure."

That filled her with pride. But one opinion wasn't always enough. "Chandler?"

She smiled. "Reece's right. You're going to win."

"I hope so." She wiped down the last table as the car doors opened, and out stepped two old women—late sixties, probably, and a younger woman with severe features. All three were dressed in business suits, which made Farrah think that this decorating committee really took things seriously, more seriously than she had originally anticipated.

The haughty-looking woman waited for the older ladies, and then the trio approached the café, eyeing it up and down. Farrah couldn't tell if their scrutinizing gazes meant they hated what they saw or liked it. Either way, it didn't matter. What did matter was what was on the inside—like with people, she supposed. What their insides were like was much more important than their outsides.

She opened the door and smiled at them. "Hello, welcome to the Lighthouse Café. Please, come inside."

The three women held clipboards that seemed to have appeared out of thin air. She hadn't noticed that they'd been holding them to begin with. Which meant that they were most definitely the decorating committee.

"We're here about the decorations," said the extreme-featured woman. It was true. Her cheekbones were sharp, her eyes dark and sparkling. Even her chin was long and pointy. "May we take a look around?"

"Of course," Farrah told them. "Please do whatever it is you need to. Can I offer you some cookies? Coffee?"

What was she saying, they didn't have cookies, did they? She shot Reece a questioning look, and the woman returned it with a subtle shake of the head.

Just as she was coming up with an excuse for the lack of cookies, the woman replied, "No, that won't be necessary. We don't need refreshments. We only need to look around."

Her nerves were on fire as the trio huddled together and slowly started critiquing, jotting down notes onto the papers attached to their clipboards.

Farrah cringed. She hoped the notes were good ones.

"We have a rubric," the woman explained over her shoulder. "Points are given based on creativity, concept, display, etc.," she said, flourishing the last word with a roll of her tongue. "In case you were wondering."

"I was," she said, a light laugh in her throat. "But don't mind us. Y'all please do what you need to."

So she tried not to pay attention. Did her best not to watch out of the corner of her eye as the three ladies walked the room, huddled together like they were in the middle of a blizzard and needed each other's body heat to keep warm.

She watched as they put their heads together, strained her ears as they whispered among themselves, nodding or shaking their heads. Her stomach quivered as they continued on this way for a solid ten minutes, slowly winding their path around the dining room, which wasn't that big, really.

But how those ladies took their time! It shocked Farrah that they could dilly and dally so much while looking at decorations. One would point to something, and the other two would nod, or shake their heads—which was the worst part to Farrah, when the head-shaking happened.

It made her soul and, for that matter, the hope in her heart wither every time she saw that. She'd put so much time and attention into the decorations that she wanted everyone to love them as much as she did. How could they not?

But after what felt like forever, the three made it all the way around. The two shorter, older women headed for the front door while the other one, who'd done all the talking, stopped in front of Farrah.

"Thank you for inviting the committee out. We have a few more places to visit, but the winner will be selected soon, and the first-place sign posted outside. That's how you'll know if you won or not."

"Oh, okay." She desperately wanted to ask who else was up for the competition. What other businesses were entering, and could she go spy on them to see if their decor was anywhere as good as hers? But instead of all that, the only thing Farrah responded with was, "Thank y'all so much for coming. I hope you enjoyed the decorations. I put my heart and soul into them."

"As well as her paycheck," Reece offered.

Farrah scowled, and Reece only winked playfully at her.

The judge cleared her throat and nodded. "Yes, thank you. Have a good day."

She joined the other judges at the front door and opened it for them. Then they were gone, having left as quickly as they arrived.

Reece tossed a towel over her shoulder. "Do you think we won?"

Farrah shook her head. "I have no idea, but I guess we'll find out soon enough."

## Chapter Fourteen

With business slowly getting back to normal, Ginny was able to focus on other things, like Savannah, when she showed up one day after lunch at the café.

She couldn't say that she was happy to see *that woman*. Who in their right mind would ever be happy to see the woman who stole your husband? But from what Farrah had told her, Ginny knew that Savannah had made her bed, and was certainly laying it.

If that wasn't justice enough, she didn't know what was.

"Do you have time to talk?" Savannah asked meekly.

"Sure," Ginny said, wiping down the last table. "Why don't we meet at the shops in a few minutes?"

"Sure. I'll see you there."

It was a beautiful day at the beach. The smallish downtown that Sugar Cove had was lined with a few shops. It wasn't anything as big as Port St. Joe, but there were a couple of gift shops that housed the usual Florida memorabilia—dehydrated baby alligator heads, bleached sun dollars and starfish, as well as wind chimes made of shells.

A small coffee shop that served beignets was her favorite. She loved a hot beignet on a cold Saturday morning, and as they were heading deeper into December, the mornings were certainly flush with cold.

The downtown streetlamps were decorated with green garland dotted with red bows as well as lights in the shape of stars and snowflakes.

At night, the sight was beautiful—all the lights and garland made everything feel Christmassy. Even during the day the decorations added a touch of charm.

It was outside of the coffee shop where Ginny found Savannah, huddled over a steaming paper cup of coffee.

"Would you like a beignet?" she asked as she grabbed the door handle.

Savannah shook her head. Worry brimmed in her eyes, and Ginny wasn't sure if she was going to add to her burden or take away from it. Either way, she was doing the right thing, she was sure of that now.

After ordering a dozen steaming hot beignets and a coffee, Ginny sat down. She pushed the box toward Savannah, and the woman shook her head.

"Take one. I can't sit and eat in front of you."

The woman frowned, but she did take one of the pieces of fried dough rolled in powdered sugar and nibble one edge.

Ginny expected it to be more tense between them, but she felt a sense of peace sitting across from the woman who had helped turn her life upside down—along with Jack, that was.

She didn't have ill feelings toward her, but she didn't exactly feel warm and cozy about Savannah, either.

"Have you been in Sugar Cove all this time?"

*That woman* shook her head. "No. I've been ho—back to Atlanta."

Her cheeks turned pink with embarrassment, and Ginny understood why. Calling Atlanta her home was an admission that it hadn't been her home before Jack had moved her there, given her a home that had never belonged to her.

"Well, you're here now."

Savannah gripped her cup of coffee so tightly that her knuckles whitened. "I...I've come for your answer on if you'd like to buy the house. I'm sure you talked to your friend and you know what's happened, but I do want you to know that the reason why I'm offering it to you is so that...well, I don't agree with what Jack did—giving me the house to begin with. It wasn't right of him, and I'm trying to make up for that."

"Buy selling it back?"

She nodded.

"You could've just given it to me to begin with."

The woman's eyes became big as plates. "Um, well, I guess that I could have, but it's just been such a whirlwind of change. Moving to a new city, settling in with my son, meeting new people. I felt like I had to give it a shot."

"Right. Had to give it a shot."

For a long time Ginny thought that part of her might feel bad for Savannah. After all, she'd been thrown into a new home and a new situation against her will, same as Ginny.

But as she stared at the woman, eyed her perfect manicure that probably cost sixty dollars, roved her gaze over the cashmere sweater and stared at the diamond earrings, Ginny didn't think that Savannah actually regretted any of it, least of all spending so much money on frivolous things.

Yes, Ginny had nice pieces of jewelry and some expensive clothes, but for the most part, she had lived frugally, buying clothes that she considered investment pieces, ones that she could wear for years to come. When she looked down at her nails now, she couldn't remember the last time that she had a professional manicure. It had been months. She'd had to placate herself with doing them herself.

So no, she didn't feel bad for what she was about to say to Savannah. "Thank you for coming all this way, and I have an answer for you."

Hope brightened her eyes. "You do?"

"Yes." Ginny bit into a beignet to buy some time. "Mm. So good." As Savannah patiently waited for an answer, Ginny finished chewing and took a last sip of coffee. "I'm not going to buy my old house back."

Savannah's jaw dropped. "But I thought that you'd want it? I thought that you'd want to move back in."

"For a long time I thought so, too. All I wanted was my old house and my old life, or what I believed was my life. But since I've moved here, to Sugar Cove, I've seen that my life can be so much more. Back in Atlanta, I would've been trapped by four walls that reminded me of Jack and our life. I would've been focusing on the past. But now I'm looking to the future. Yes, it's a bit different than I imagined, but it's one I'm excited for, all the same."

Savannah was quiet for a long minute. She stared at her coffee before she said quietly, "I'm sorry for all the pain and hurt that I've caused you. I truly am. I know that I can't take back what I've done—"

"No, you can't," Ginny interrupted.

Her eyes flashed up and she nodded, swallowing. "I know, and I hope that in the future, I'm a better person, that I do more and don't hurt people the way that I have. You didn't deserve what happened to you."

"No, I didn't. But I also think that if it hadn't been you, it may have been someone else. I think Jack would've been drawn away from me no matter what. I really do. As much as I hate to say that, you're about as special as any woman would've been, anyone that he could live out a magical fantasy with so that he had a secret life on the side."

Her jaw fell, and Savannah scoffed. "You're saying that me and my son aren't special? That we didn't mean anything to Jack?"

"I think you became special to him, yes. But if you'd married him and stayed with him, your relationship would've eventually turned out just like ours." She leaned forward, her elbows on the table. "You see, the one person Jack truly loved above all others was himself, and I don't think anyone could change that about him—not even you."

Savannah sat back in shock. Her eyes darted wildly around, and her mouth opened and shut as if she was trying to think of something to say, but no words came.

Ginny almost hated telling these things to Savannah, but this woman wasn't an innocent bystander. She had willingly gotten involved with a married man and had birthed his child. She deserved the truth, and there was no point in sugar coating it.

"So no, I won't be taking the house," she confirmed again.

Savannah threw her head back and laughed. "That's just fine, because I wouldn't sell it to you anyway."

Savannah pushed back her chair, the sound of the feet scraping against the wooden patio grating to Ginny's ears. She shouldered her purse. "I hope you have a great life," sarcastically as she stormed off.

As Ginny watched *that woman* slide into her car and drive off, a faint smile quirked on her lips. "I will have a great life," she murmured. "I certainly will."

# Chapter Fifteen

## FARRAH

When Farrah entered the dining room a few days later, the last thing that she expected to see was some sort of sign outside.

"What could that be?"

At first she thought that perhaps Savannah, in her anger at Ginny for not wanting to buy her old house back, had placed some sort of nasty signage out front. Or worse, Jack's ex-wife had upped her attacks and wasn't just spreading lies about food poisoning; she was now announcing in bold letters that the café had poisoned people.

But that wasn't what greeted her when she opened the door to get a closer look.

The sign that was staked into the small patch of grass outside the lighthouse didn't say anything about food poisoning or any other nasty thing.

In fact, it wasn't anything nasty at all. Instead it read:

*First Place Winner in the Sugar Cove Christmas Decorating Contest.*

Farrah screamed. It couldn't be helped. She shrieked with happiness as tears leaked down her face. What was wrong with her?

What was wrong, she realized, was that for the past weeks she'd been holding on to a world of hurt and anger, judgment and frustration—at herself, at Brad.

She'd been so convinced that he was cheating because she'd wanted to be, Farrah realized. She had wanted her husband to be cheating because she'd never truly gotten over his cheating from the past. She hadn't worked through that hurt the way she should have. Instead she let it fester inside of her, becoming an infection that burst open when she spotted the first reason to allow it to do so.

And what had she done then? She'd ran. She'd fled from her life and tucked herself under Ginny's wing to hide out. She hadn't even told her husband where she was going. She'd only driven as fast as she could to get as far away as possible.

So when Brad had said that he might have cancer, she'd felt even worse. How could she turn her back on him during his time of need? It was easy when you told yourself that he wasn't faithful and that he deserved to be treated this way.

But did he?

Brad didn't rush off to some mistress for comfort. He'd come to her. He'd tracked Farrah to the beach and had told her that he needed her. *Her.* If he'd been cheating, wouldn't he have gone to his mistress, rested his head on her bosom for comfort?

He certainly wouldn't have uprooted his life for the likes of Sugar Cove.

Which meant that in reality, Brad wasn't being unfaithful. Yes, he'd done so in the past, but he'd truly tried to be a better person. He'd tried to make up for his past mistakes, and Farrah had thought that she'd forgiven him, but deep down she hadn't. She didn't owe Brad anything. He'd walked out on their marriage first. But he'd also returned, and she loved him. He loved her, too. That was what hurt the most—that she loved him so much.

She had work to do. A lot of work when it came to trusting Brad again. But she thought that it could be done—in fact, she knew it could be if she allowed herself to admit the truth of what was in her heart—that the trust needed to be rebuilt, and she had to acknowledge that she'd been crushed in the first place. Telling Ginny had been a good first step toward her goal.

A world of emotions sliced through her as Farrah stared at the sign, the goal that she had worked so hard for, if nothing else but to make Ginny proud of her, and to have earned her stay at the lighthouse.

Yes, it was obvious that she was under everyone's feet there, but no one had complained to Farrah, and for that she was grateful.

The door burst open, and Reece said, breathless, "What is it? What's the matter?"

Tears were leaking from her eyes now. "Look," she choked out. "Look and see."

She pointed to the sign and Reece's gaze followed. Her hands flew to her cheeks, and she shouted, "Yes! Let me get Mama."

Ginny was outside a few seconds later. She studied the sign for a moment before opening her arms and pulling Farrah into a hug. "You did it. You won!"

"I couldn't have done it without y'all," Farrah told her, holding her friend tight. "The three of us did this together."

A car rolling down the street slowed in front of the lighthouse. A woman in the passenger seat lowered her window and shouted, "Congratulations!"

"Thank you," Ginny told her.

The stranger's gaze washed up and down the lighthouse. "You know, I haven't been to your restaurant before."

Farrah chuckled. "You should come in. My best friend, Ginny, serves the best food around."

"I'll just do that," she replied. "I'll see y'all for lunch."

As the car drove off, Ginny lifted her brows. "You know, this sign might be all the advertising we need to squash the rumor that Ellen started. If that's the case, I owe you my livelihood."

She scoffed. "You don't owe me anything, Ginny Rigby."

As they embraced once again, Farrah couldn't help feeling elated at this victory. Yes, she'd managed to accomplish what she'd wanted. There wasn't anything left for her to do in Sugar Cove except talk to Brad.

*　*　*

She called him after lunch, and they agreed to meet on the beach at sunset. Farrah put on a pair of loose-fitting pants and a white, long-sleeved blouse. She made sure that her makeup looked nice, and she pulled her hair back into a ponytail, noticing that she really needed to get her roots touched up.

It was funny. If she'd been back in Atlanta, they would've already been dyed. But here in Sugar Cove, life was slower, and things that seemed so important in the city sat on the back burner here, allowing other things that sometimes got overlooked to come to the forefront.

She spotted Brad as he parked his SUV along the strip of a parking lot for the daily beachgoers. He looked handsome as he brushed his hair to one side, and Farrah wondered when she'd stopped noticing how handsome her husband was. Was it when he'd hurt her all those years ago? Had that been the beginning of the end?

Well, it certainly hadn't helped, had it?

His gaze roved the beach until he spotted her waving. He broke into a smile and jogged down the small dune at the back of the parking lot and over the sugary sand to meet her.

"Sorry I'm late," he said, kissing her cheek.

"It's fine. It gave me a few minutes to think."

He rubbed the back of his neck. It was what Brad did when he was worried. She supposed that between her behavior and the cancer, he'd had a lot to think about.

"Shall we walk?" she said, pointing down the beach.

"Sure."

There weren't many people out this time of year, when the weather turned cold. It was mostly locals out running or people walking their dogs on the sand.

The sun was setting on the horizon, washing the sky in brilliant pink and orange. It was a sight that Farrah had tattooed in her mind time and time again. She loved seeing the sunset. It made her heart light.

"I heard that y'all won the decorating contest," he said.

"Yes," she replied, surprised by that. "How'd you know?"

"I drove by," he admitted bashfully.

"Oh. Well, it's a small town. You can't keep secrets forever."

"No, I suppose you can't."

"Listen, Brad, I wanted to talk to you."

"I gathered that," he teased.

She sighed. Why was this harder than it should be? "I'm going to admit some things, and I don't need you to tell me that you told me so."

He pressed a hand to his heart. "Scout's honor that I won't."

She eyed him warily. "Promise?"

"I promise, Farrah."

"Okay." She cleared her throat, trying to get rid of the knot that was suddenly lodged in it. "I guess that...well, you see, the thing is..." Jeez. Why was it so hard to start this sentence? "Okay, well. Here's the thing: I never really forgave you for the affair. I thought that I had, but I was wrong. Instead of working through all that hurt, I stuffed it way down, deep inside, thinking it was better to ignore it than it was to deal with it. So when I saw that text, it snapped something inside of me, and the only thing that I could do was run."

"Farrah, I swear, that text was about your birthday party. It wasn't about anything else."

"I believe you." She paused and turned to face him. He did the same. "I choose to believe you. I've misjudged and distrusted you, which to be honest, I feel perfectly right in feeling. You broke my trust once, in a terrible way. I choose to stay then. But I shouldn't have run off now. I should've dealt with our problems years ago, when they happened, instead of burying my fear way down where it could grow. It wasn't fair to just up and leave without letting you explain, and it wasn't fair to me."

"Sometimes," he said tenderly, "it's hard to know what's fair until you're looking at it from the outside."

"That's true. So very, very true." She inhaled a deep breath, preparing herself for the next part of her speech. "When you told me about the cancer, part of me didn't want to believe it. Part of me wanted to think that it was just an excuse to get me back to Atlanta. But I know you wouldn't do that."

"I hope so," he replied with an eye roll.

She squeezed his bicep. "I do. I know it. *Now*. I've had to look deep into my heart in order to be able to accept it, but now I'm sure, and I'm ready to move ahead."

He cocked a brow. "I hope by when you say, 'Move ahead,' you're talking about us."

"Yes, I am." She smiled up at him, remembering what it was like to smile at him at their wedding so many years ago. "I want to come home. It's time for me to leave Sugar Cove and go back with you to our life. I'm sorry that I left like I did. I'll never do it again."

Brad folded his arms. "Wait just a minute now. You can't just snap your fingers and expect that everything is forgotten."

His words jolted her. "I don't."

"There are going to be some ground rules to this."

He was teasing her. "Like what?" she asked, playing along.

"Like if you ever feel like I'm doing something behind your back, no matter what it is, you come to me first before you pack a bag and jump into your car. Got it?"

She suppressed a smile. "Got it. What else?"

"Second, if I tell you that something's true, I need you to promise to at least attempt to believe me."

"I will. I'm giving you my trust."

"Good. Now, what else?" he asked the sky before snapping his fingers. "And there's one more condition."

"What's that?"

He stepped in, closing the distance between them. "That we seal these promises with a kiss."

She grinned as she curled her fingers into the front of his shirt. "Deal accepted."

When Brad kissed her, any doubts in Farrah's mind about him and their future vanished. The one thought she did have was, *I'm home.*

## Chapter Sixteen

The week leading up to Christmas was extraordinarily busy. The sign posting that the Lighthouse Café had won the Sugar Cove decorating contest had indeed generated buzz and delivered new customers to them. In fact, there were so many that on several occasions Ginny'd had to turn people away from the dining room, but she'd made up for it by offering folks take-out boxes full of food.

She just hated losing a customer.

It also turned out that as old customers spotted new ones filling up their old parking spots, they started to return, too. So in no time, the damage that Ellen had done was erased from everyone's minds.

Except Ginny's.

But there wasn't any time to think about that now, because it was the night of the Sugar Cove Christmas Ball, and Ginny was putting the finishing touches on her look. Her makeup was perfect. Reece had helped pin up her hair, and her dress, though old, was regal enough for royalty.

The dark green satin gown had draping chiffon straps, a sweetheart neckline, and a skirt that hugged her hips as it fell to the floor. It was elegant and also beautifully made, shimmering as she walked.

She found a pair of emerald and diamond studs that were an old birthday present from Jack, and she pushed them into her ears and took a step back, admiring her reflection.

"Oh, Mama, you look beautiful," Reece said with a sigh. "You're going to be the most beautiful belle at the ball."

Ginny's gaze washed over Reece in her knee-length red dress. "I'm not sure if I'll be the only one. You look beautiful, too. Ted's not going to know what to do with himself when he sees you."

Her daughter blushed. "Stop."

Both women laughed as they finished getting ready, and when Aiden arrived to pick her up, he let out a wolf whistle at the sight of her.

"If I'd known that when I asked you, I'd be bringing a debutante, I would've worn my tux," he said, eyes twinkling.

"Stop." She swatted at him. "You know that I'm not like that."

"I know, but you look beautiful." He stepped up and brushed his lips over her cheek, which made heat flush her neck. "I'm going to be the luckiest guy at the ball."

She smiled as he took her hand and led her to his SUV, where her chariot awaited.

\* \* \*

The restaurant where the ball was being held was decked out in so many Christmas lights that they instantly warmed her skin. The recessed lights were dimmed, but the twinkling ones that were wrapped around every pole and draped atop every surface sparkled with white light.

Frosted garland dotted with red berries and brown pine cones hung from the rafters, making the entire room feel like a winter wonderland.

It seemed like most of Sugar Cove was in attendance. Customers that she knew waved when they spotted her, and people were slowly making their way to the dance floor.

"Care to dance?" Aiden asked.

Under the lights she got her first good look at him. He wore a dark suit with a dark green tie that complimented his blue eyes. The corners of his eyes crinkled when he smiled, which made her heart flutter.

As he reached for her hand, she said, "I'd love to dance."

So they did. They moved slowly to the music, and she pressed her cheek to his, inhaling his briny and leather scent.

"You smell nice," he murmured.

She chuckled.

"What?"

"I was just thinking the same thing about you."

He laughed. "Great minds, and all that."

"Yep," she murmured. "Great minds."

They danced for two more songs until they took a break. In the throng Ginny spotted Farrah and Brad. She was relieved that her best friend had decided to go home. Not because she was tired of Farrah being there. No, it was more like Ginny knew that Farrah belonged back in Atlanta with her husband.

"Let's go say hi," she said to Aiden, pulling him through the crowd.

They spoke to the couple for a few minutes before Ginny spotted Chandler with Hudson, and Reece and Ted. Her girls were both smiling up at the men they cared about. Chandler would soon be married, and Ginny didn't know where Reece's relationship with Ted would wind up, but she had a feeling that it would be someplace good.

"Would you like a glass of punch?" Ginny asked Aiden.

"I can get us two cups."

"No." She pressed a hand to his shoulder. "I don't mind. I'll be right back."

She instantly regretted offering to get the punch because standing at the table was none other than Ellen. Her heart sank at the sight of the woman in her Christmas gold shimmery wrap dress.

Ellen spotted Ginny and her lip curled.

"Merry Christmas," Ginny said.

Ellen dragged her gaze up and down Ginny, and then back again. "Hm," was all she said.

Anger stirred in her because honestly, Ellen had no right to act like Ginny was in the wrong. She hadn't made up the rumors about her own café, and she had trusted Vera's information.

"Told your boyfriend to talk to me, did you?"

Ginny cringed. "Um, no, I didn't. But if he did, I'm sure it was for good reason."

Ellen scoffed. "Good reason? I don't have any idea what you're talking about."

*Sure* she didn't. "Excuse me, I'd like to get some punch."

Aiden's ex moved aside, but she lingered at the table while Ginny poured the drinks, staring her down the whole time. It was obvious that the real estate agent wanted to make Ginny uncomfortable, but that wasn't going to work.

She whistled "Walking in a Winter Wonderland" while pouring the drinks. The whole time Ellen stared daggers at her, but Ginny didn't care. She had won. Her business had survived, and in fact it was doing better than ever. Plus, she had Aiden. He wasn't going anywhere.

While she was pouring a second glass, a man on the other side of the table, facing the opposite direction, bumped into it, causing the punch to slosh and the glasses to rattle.

Ginny wasn't sure if he was drunk or not, but he was certainly happy. She quickly finished pouring, and with both drinks in hand, she gave Ellen one more, "Merry Christmas," before walking away.

Just as she reached Aiden, a huge crash sounded behind her. She whirled around to see that the man who had bumped into the table before had whirled around. His mouth was open in shock at the sight before him.

The huge punch bowl had tipped over, and all the liquid had splashed onto Ellen, who stood drenched from the waist down. Punch dripped off her dress, pooling around her very soaked feet.

Ginny didn't laugh, but she couldn't help but think that it was nothing better than just deserts as Ellen stormed off and out the front door.

"Good riddance," Aiden murmured.

She toasted him to that. "I thought that you weren't going to say anything to Ellen. She told me that you spoke to her."

He shrugged. "What was I supposed to do? Let my ex-wife scare off my girlfriend?"

A jolt skated down her spine. "Girlfriend? Am I your girlfriend now?"

"Well, aren't you?"

A wide smile broke out over her face. "Yeah, I guess I am."

And it was then, under the Christmas lights, that Aiden cupped Ginny's cheek and kissed her, making every muscle in her body tighten, all the way to her toes.

"Merry Christmas," he murmured when the kiss broke.

"Merry Christmas," she replied, knowing that this Christmas would be one of the best she'd ever had.

# A LIGHTHOUSE CHRISTMAS

\* \* \*

Thank you for reading A LIGHTHOUSE CHRISTMAS. I hope you enjoyed it! If you love the ladies in Sugar Cove, be sure to tell your friends.

The best way to learn about new books is through word-of-mouth, so please spread the word if you love spending time in Sugar Cove!

Hudson and Chandler are getting married! Order your copy of A LIGHTHOUSE WEDDING so that you don't miss one minute of the Rigby's lives.

To keep up with what's going on in Sugar Cove and to learn about other releases that Bebe Reed may be having, be sure to join her newsletter.

You can sign up here: https://bebereed.com/

Printed in Great Britain
by Amazon